Th.

This is probably not the opportune time to point out that I'm not all that great with kids. My memories of being one don't seem to square up with how they react to things, or how their parents treat them like poorly-constructed Fabergé eggs. I do my best, and then do my best to get out of the situation ASAP.

My niece shuffled over to the seat, tried once or twice to speak, then she curled up in a ball in a corner. Terrified.

I leaned forward and gave her hair a little tousle. "Sarah, you came in here to tell me something. What is it?"

"The house," she whispered, "it's haunted."

"Oh, honey, ghosts look scary, but as soon as the lights are on, they go away."

"No. They're here all the time. They...they..." She clammed up for a second, but her eyes were wide and didn't blink, staring past me into the middle-distance, "they whisper. And they walk, outside in the yard."

"You can hear them?"

"Every night."

"Now this is very important, Sarah. What do they whisper about?"

She hesitated, and then said a word with almost no breath behind it. "Daddy. They say he's in trouble. They say he's going to die."

Yup, should have stayed at the Airport Hilton. Dammit.

"If I hired you, would you find the ghosts and make them go away?"

I made a show of considering it. "Do you have a quarter?"

"No." She dug around in the pockets of her PJ pants and produced a five spot, "All I got's this."

"Okay, you got yourself a detective."

Also by J. Daniel Sawyer

The Antithesis Progression
Predestination
Free Will
Avarice (forthcoming)

The Clarke Lantham Mysteries
And Then She Was Gone
A Ghostly Christmas Present
Smoke Rings
Silent Victor
He Ain't Heavy (forthcoming)

Standalone Works
Down From Ten
Ideas, Inc.
Suave Rob's Double-X Derring-Do (forthcoming)

Nonfiction
Making Tracks: A Writer's Guide to Producing Audiobooks
Science Fiction Weaponry: A Guide for Writers (with Mary Mason)
Throwing Lead: A Writer's Guide to Firearms and the People Who Use Them (with Mary Mason)

Collections
Sculpting God: Bedtime Stories for Adults
Frock Coat Dreams: Romances, Nightmares, and Fancies from the Steampunk Fringe
Tales of a Lombard Alchemist, Volume 1 (forthcoming)

A GHOSTLY CHRISTMAS PRESENT

A CLARKE LANTHAM MYSTERY

J. Daniel Sawyer

AWP Mystery
a division of AWP Books
© 2011 J. Daniel Sawyer
All Rights Reserved
ISBN-13: 978-1466465145

Cover Illustration by Kitty NicIaian
Book Design by Kitty NicIaian
Back Cover Photograph ©2008, Dave Nakayama,
Used Under Creative Commons Attribution 2.0
Snowflake photographs taken Wilson Bentley,
circa 1885-1931. Public domain
Christmas tree photograph, ©2005 Henryk Zychowski, Used Under
Creative Commons Attribution 3.0, courtesy Wikicommons

First publication: December, 2010

Dedication

For the world's most entertaining traveling companion

The Phantom slowly, gravely, silently approached. When it came near him, Scrooge bent down upon his knee; for in the very air through which this Spirit moved it seemed to scatter gloom and mystery. It was shrouded in a deep black garment, which concealed its head, its face, its form, and left nothing of it visible...

Charles Dickens
A Christmas Carol
1843

6:00 PM, SUNDAY

CLANG.

IT'S A SPECIAL SOUND TO HEAR ON Christmas Eve morning, more distinctive than any Salvation Army bell. Immediately before you hear it, some gruff guard is liable to bellow out an "all clear"—but I wouldn't count on it. Like cops, prison guards come in two flavors: the compassionate ones that wanted to make the world a better place, and the abused kids that grew up to be bullies.

Cops—well, cops in well-run departments—tend to tilt toward the former. Prison guards tend to tilt the other way. So if your hand gets crushed when the gate closes, it's more entertainment for them.

They sure as hell didn't know what to do with me. They kept looking at me and saying "you don't belong here," even during the strip search.

Of course, in this podunk Twin Peaks wannabe town, the sheriff's deputy that threw me in here claimed they didn't have any room left in the holding tank because of too many drunks. Besides, I used to be a cop. I'd be fine in lockup, right?

Yeah, right.

Naturally, they stuck me with the big mean-looking dude

who would've been called "Bubba" in any decent prison movie. That he introduced himself as "Manny," and had about a third grade education, gave the whole enterprise just enough pathetic to keep me fighting back my menacing laughter.

"You an' me's cellies now, boy." On anyone else, that squeaky voice would be a dead giveaway that his balls were just starting to drop, except this guy was easily twenty five and—judging by the swastika on his shaved head and the Black Power tattoo on his left shoulder—a confused victim of identity politics. Hearing him schlep up behind me like he expected me to beg his favor wasn't one of the more companionable roommate experiences I've ever had, and I went to school at U.C. Santa Cruz. "You's gonna be my good boy and I'll make sure life is real purdy for ya."

I heard fly buttons pop open behind me. In jail for fifteen minutes, and I already got an overgrown third grader trying to play doctor with me. Joy to the world, my cell-mate wants to come.

I stepped back from the bars until I bumped into him and said, in my best quavery scared-as-hell coward voice, "You promise? Thanks, man." I reached back 'til I found his hip, snaked my hand down to his balls, and got a good handful. Then, I gave them a nice squeeze and a slow twist.

"Ooh, that's right boy, jes...ow! What the..." I clamped down so hard he couldn't do anything but grab the bunk and try to stay upright so I didn't take his nuts off if he fell backward.

Another really good twist, and a little more pressure, I turned around to make sure I had his undivided attention. "Oh come on now, Immanuel. I'm not your captive." Yeah, I was in that kind of mood. Endless Christmas music in hotel lobbies does that to me.

He squeezed out a "Huh?" between groans and failed

attempts to scream.

"So here's the deal. We're gonna be pals. You and me, all the way. But I ain't your catcher, or I'll take these," I gave his jewels another twist, "and make 'em into a necklace. You got me?"

Staring down a guy four inches taller and a couple hundred pounds heavier than you isn't exactly a trick you learn in kindergarten. Time on the beat has its advantages.

He gritted his teeth. Sweat beads coming up on his head now. Face red as Rudolph's nose. Kept him in too much pain for the adrenaline to help him any. Good thing too—he could've made a smoothie out of me without trying. But after this much pain, I was banking that he'd need to sleep off the testicle torsion before he got his revenge. A bit of a gamble: there weren't any scheduled activities for a couple hours yet, so I was stuck in here with him.

And he wasn't answering my question.

"I said," I scooted close enough that he tried to retreat. *Coach, we have a first down.* "Do you got me?"

He still didn't say anything.

"Look, if you don't answer me, I might just have to blow you. And I haven't had breakfast yet today." I squeezed a little harder. Much harder and I might actually break something. "So, you got me?"

"Yeah, yeah, goddammit, I got ya," he squeaked.

"Good man." I let go all at once and gave him a gentle push. He collapsed on the bed with his hands cradling his genitals, and curled into a fetal position with his ass hanging out of his drawers.

Well, there was gonna be a full moon tonight. Might as well start early.

I turned my attention back to the view out the bars and ran over my less-than-dignified Christmas Eve.

Count on the idiot named "Clarke Lantham" to provoke a cop just because the cop was a prick. Count on him to do it in a state where his lawyer wasn't a member of the bar, and the only person he could call was the brother whom he'd deliberately avoided telling he was in town. And then, count on that same self-professed idiot to do it all when he was trying to get home by rental car to see to a business emergency.

Yeah, there's some things only the ass-end of a set of prison bars can teach you. Chief among them being: "Don't try to find a way out of Sea-Tac through the suburbs when a snowstorm closes the airport."

Granted, it isn't the kind of fortune-cookie proverb that's likely to come in handy every day, but if the waitress at the Hilton had been kind enough to scribble it on my receipt this morning I'd be at least a whole mile south of the airport by now, without having the extra helping of testicles before lunch.

If I'm gonna be honest, though—and, when you're standing in a prison cell with a four-hundred-pound six-foot-seven cellie snoring like a polar bear with flu, there isn't much sense in creative self-deception—my assistant Rachael pegged my first mistake during our phone meeting yesterday. Her typically genteel appraisal of my situation ran something along the lines of "Jesus Christ, Lantham, only you would go to an insurance convention in Seattle in the middle of inheritance season and not check the weather report. How the hell did you stay in business before you hired me?"

She was gonna crap fresh grapefruits when she heard about my current predicament. Top of my agenda was not letting her find out yet—last thing I needed this morning was guff from my twenty-year-old underpaid gothy employee. Particularly when she was right about it.

Now I just had to wait for my brother-who-wishes-he-wasn't to show up, and ponder the meaning of

Christmas—which was ostensibly coming tomorrow, though the weather seemed to have different ideas.

I can sum up the meaning of Christmas in one word:

Crunch.

Otherwise known as "the sound you don't want to hear when you're in a car."

For me, the holiday season is full of little surprises from Santa like that one. Most years, I'm home in Oakland, and December in Oakland is just *miserable*. The worst thing you've ever seen. I mean, in bad years we'll get ten or twelve inches of rain over the month, and the thermometer will drop to almost forty degrees during the day—sometimes, I shit you not, we'll even get some frost overnight. It's a horror show for traffic—the interstates can get so bad that it might take more than an hour to make the fifty miles from Oakland to Los Gatos. Really rough, right? If you live in the Bay Area, you learn to hate it.

So, really, the thing about winter is that, around the Bay, you kinda forget what the thing about winter is. You think about the rain and the minor bump in traffic. You think about what a pain in the ass it is to have to remember gloves if you're going out after dark and intend to spend any amount of time outside—because, really, who goes outside in winter after sunset for any reason other than to get from the car to a club? You get to think that these kind of piss-ant conditions actually constitute "bad weather." You forget that something called "snow" exists in the rest of the country.

With that in mind, you probably think the reason that the side of my car was mushroomed in from a broadside in the Seattle slush was that I blew through a signal at ten miles an hour on slick ice, right?

Yeah, you'd think that. It hurts when reality doesn't cooperate with prejudice, isn't it? I run into that all the time.

Sorry for the surly mood. It's been a hell of a few days. But rest assured, I keep my cold-weather knives sharp with twice-annual refresher courses at Infineon. Have to. My PI license means I can operate anywhere in California, and you never know when someone's going to call you up to Dodge Ridge or Tahoe to find their missing cat.

So yeah, I'm spoiled rotten, but I also live in California, so I pay a lot for my spoiling. And I'd have an excuse if I drove like crap in the snow, even though I don't. The mooks up in Washington, though, who get snow at least once a year, act like they've never seen the stuff. White flakes start falling from the sky and they all rush out to the store at sixty miles-an-hour to buy God a fresh bottle of Head and Shoulders.

Of all the sounds that can tickle your ears when you're in the car, "crunch" is right up there with "boom" for ones you don't want to hear. But it's *really* not a sound you want to hear when you're sitting at a stop-light on a road in suboptimal driving conditions, or when it's accompanied by the sound of a honking horn and a pair of high-beams embedding themselves in your driver-side window frame three inches from your head. About the only good thing that can come out of a sound like that is the relief when you realize the truck hadn't been going fast enough to actually push you out of the driver's seat.

But the local cops don't see it that way when they get a look at your out-of-state license, which is why they had me leaning against their car while they took my statement, debating whether they should charge me with reckless endangerment.

"You know that it's against the law to drive so fast that you put other people in danger, don't you?" Officer Bellman said. He was easily the more senior of the two, in his mid forties and none-too-happy to be out on a day like this. Up here, they called places like Vancouver and Tacoma "cities," and this guy had the big-fish/small-pond thing going behind the coffee-stained breath that he insisted on sharing with me.

"What part of 'He lost control and damn near killed me' doesn't compute?"

Bellman hitched his belt up, spread his legs a little apart, and swaggered up so he was close enough to kiss me. I resisted making the obvious joke. "I've got you on misdemeanor endangerment, buster, this ain't the time to go pissing me off."

"Look," I put my hands between my butt and the car so I wouldn't be tempted to shove him off me, "I don't *actually* think you're an idiot. But it's cold out, and your breath says you've only had one pot of coffee today. I'm just saying you need more antifreeze if you're going to expect your brain to work when you're out this weather."

"That's it. Turn around and spread 'em."

I shrugged and did what he said. Yeah, I know it's dumb to antagonize the cops, but at that point I didn't give a damn. At that point, I was getting a kick out of the fantasy of suing this joker for false arrest just so I could be the cherry on top of his Sunday the same way he was currently dolloping whipped turds on top of mine.

So, there I was in the klink, waiting for my kid brother Sam—who should have been called Smeagol—to show up and post for me. Then I'd have to stay with him over the holiday until the arraignment on Tuesday. Christmas with this branch of the family? Even Dante never thought of that one.

I ground my teeth together. It should have been a nice day of getting slowly sodomized by the gods of Seattle traffic. Rachael had called this morning to tell that there was a problem with Southland, and it was no good going into it on the phone because they wouldn't settle for dealing with my assistant, no matter what. No, they wouldn't talk on the phone. Yes, it had to be in person. No, she didn't have any other details.

Which meant I couldn't wait for the airport to open back up, so I'd rented a subcompact and tried heading south on my own. A thirteen hour drive in good weather, so I'd probably get home about the time the weather broke and I could just take a two hour flight, but at least I wouldn't be sitting around the bloody Airport Hilton cooling my heels. I'd comforted myself with the knowledge that at least the conference netted me a handful of leads for regular insurance gigs. Steady work is the unicorn of the self-employed, and there ain't a one of us who's virginal in any sense.

Sam showed up before Manny could find his way back to the land of the wakeful. Just as well—I didn't fancy trying to convince him he needed to buy me flowers before we got serious about our enforced cohabitation.

But Sam I hadn't seen in more than ten years, and I can't say they sat well on him. He was standing in the waiting area past the checkpoint in the front office. An couple inches taller than me at six five, thin like a toothpick that hadn't been eating properly. At about thirty-two he was three years younger, and he had smoker's lines starting to come in around his eyes and jawline. Last time I saw him was before his wedding. Now he looked like someone who spent a good part of his time playing chewing tobacco to Lady Luck.

"Clarke." He nodded, but barely. Didn't stick out a hand, but he did carry one of my bags. It was more sociable than I expected.

"Sam." I returned the nod.

A banker in the day time for one of those little independent banks that customers run to when the big banks fail, his Bentley said money almost as much as his house did—a house that took us an hour and a half to find in the ice and snow-covered hill maze.

No chauffeur, which half-surprised me. He set the bags in

the back seat and flipped an effete hand to the passenger door, then shambled around to his side, crouching, on the edge of a flinch, like someone used to being hunted. Not the same guy who'd thrown me out of his life once upon a time—on the upside, at least he came and bailed me out.

We didn't slip-slide all over the road—snow tires. Said he kept a spare set in the garage for days like this. He seemed to know which roads to drive to avoid the idiots.

"You still with Oakland?" He asked.

He was still on speaking terms with our parents, so he should have known better. Cheap jab. I played it straight. "No. Private now."

"Hmph. Interesting work?"

"Keeps me busy."

"Hmph." Aside from a little bit of the perfunctory tour-guide routine, he didn't say anything much for the rest of the drive. Then again, we'd said all there was to say twelve years ago.

"Well, here we are." He squeezed it out of a tight throat, like he was constipated and trying to get things moving. "Built in the twenties. Three governors lived here after they retired."

"Peachy."

The house was Gothic Revival—high pitched roofs, big lawn, hill, winding drive, nasty-looking wrought-iron gates. The kind of place you might see in a costume drama, or a *Rocky Horror* remake, all buried in white.

The reception inside the house was slightly less chilly. I guess upper class manners demand a hell of a hospitality act.

He had me set my things in the foyer, then showed me personally to the dining room where the family seemed to be just finishing up with dinner.

"Clarke!" Samantha—yes, Sam's wife was also called Sam; my brother came up short in a lot of areas, but height and narcissism were two in which he measured up well enough to make a try for the record books—welcomed me with a just-barely-too-warm hug that, along with her parents sitting indifferently at the other end of the long table, made it painfully easy to remember why I hadn't been invited to the wedding. She broke the hug and held on to my arms for a minute, looking at me as if she were trying to see whether I'd changed at all, and in what direction.

Her face was all smiles, but her eyes had a hint of the same hunted look I saw on my brother.

She turned to the rest of the table. "Mom, Dad, you remember Clarke."

Her father grunted a perfunctory greeting. Her mother showed a tad more hospitality, but only as far as etiquette demanded. There are some people who serve as the perfect moral barometer: If they approve of you, it's time to do some serious soul searching.

"Tom. Edith. Good to see you're doing well." I nodded to each of them and smiled a bit, not insincerely. If they were still alive, it went a long way to explaining Sam's bearing.

I turned my attention to the three kids. Twin twelve-year-old boys—the product of Samantha's youthful rebellion against the silver handcuffs she'd been born into—and a younger girl, nine or ten if memory served. Even if the trademark pokey ears didn't mark her out as a Lantham, the way she fidgeted under the burden of formality certainly did. "Let's see if I remember." I made a show of squinting hard to remember, "Jimmy, who hates chocolate, Albert, who loves peas, and...Sarah," I looked at her plate, "Who can't stand potatoes."

The boys weren't very impressed, but Sarah seemed to appreciate that someone noticed her. That figured. Sam might be aging fast, but he hadn't changed much otherwise.

"Who are you?" she asked, all narrow eyes and suspicion like she was having trouble placing me on the friend/foe graph.

"This is your uncle Clarke from San Francisco," Samantha said.

I managed not to mutter "Oakland." In this part of the world, it was a meaningless distinction—one city, you were a fag, in the other, you were a gangbanger. All things considered, and despite my adventure in prison earlier today, I'd rather be thought light in the loafers than fast on the trigger. Not that I expected these kids to have picked up that much fine-grained prejudice yet.

Jimmy said "hi" with a tone of relief that only comes from having endured too much attention from micro-managing grandparents. Albert, already jockeying to be the pack alpha, stood, sized me up, then walked over and offered a hand, which I shook.

"So what do you do in San Francisco?"

"I'm a private detective."

His eyes did a convincing impersonation of saucers. "Like *The Maltese Falcon*?"

"Something like that."

"Caught any serial killers?"

"Honey," Samantha interposed herself between us, "Your uncle Clarke's had a long day, and needs to eat something before you..."

"No, no, that's fine." Damn the fact that it wasn't my house, I've got a thing about kids that are forced into good behavior. "Ask me anything you like, but dinner sounds good."

"You like pheasant?"

"At this point I'd eat a raw rhinoceros."

"Cynthia!" Samantha clapped her hands like she was calling a dog. A maid, probably a grad student and wearing the most genuine smile I'd seen all evening, and followed by the sound of bawdy laughter, poked her head through what turned out to be the kitchen door.

"Yes?"

"Bring a plate for our guest?"

"Certainly, ma'am." She disappeared again.

The dining room was a cherry-wood finished affair with a long, formal table set without a tablecloth. No centerpiece to prevent the diners from seeing each other—judging by the seating arrangements, this was probably so that the kids wouldn't have anything to hide behind while being scrutinized by the adults on the other side of the table. The head was empty, and I was tired enough that my inhibitions were riding pretty thin, so I didn't quite manage to squelch a very childish impulse.

"I wonder if I...no, never mind."

"What?" Samantha asked.

"Well...no, never mind, really, it's stupid."

"We haven't seen you in years. There aren't any stupid questions." She seemed to mean it, despite the huffs of derision from both her parents and from her husband, still standing in the doorway behind me.

"There's just always something I've wanted to do..."

Without asking permission, mostly because I couldn't have stomached even *more* politeness, I swept up to the head of the table and sat down at the cleared space that my brother would normally have occupied. I perched my elbows on the table and tented my hands, drumming my fingertips against each other. "Thank you all for joining me," I said in my best Boris Karloff, "There has been...a murder."

Childish, yeah. But I couldn't help myself. I stood up again before anyone could say anything, and took a seat down at the ass end of the table in a blank spot next to the kids.

"Wha..." Sam started.

"Nothing. I've just always wanted to do that."

"Whatever." He left the room rather than take his own seat for some dinner.

Once I'd taken the first bite of my asparagus, Albert considered the interrogation officially open, and in between my swallows of a very nice Pinot Grigio and nibbles from the unfortunate bird on my plate, he started grilling me about my glamorous life as a private eye. When I didn't make him shut up, the other kids joined in post haste.

You get used to that kind of thing in my job, if not with this level of enthusiasm, so I gave them a Bowdlerized version of last year's New Year's Eve party—enough action and intrigue to get my niece and two nephews excited, hopefully not enough to give them nightmares or spank material. My sister-in-law seemed to approve, and invited me along to help bed the kids down in the family room. Clustered around the hearth, their annual "sleep under the tree and try to catch Santa Claus" tradition. They kept me telling stories for a couple hours before I finally managed to beg off and go back to my room to check my email.

Seemed like a big house for a family of five, even with the parents-in-law and the house staff—three of them, near as I could figure. The guest room where they stuck me was big enough to hold my whole office suite and a small coffee stand. Sam had done alright for himself, and though I found his paranoid tics unsettling, I couldn't bring myself to feel sorry for him. On anyone else it would've looked pitiful. On him, it felt like justice.

Not that I'm one to hold a grudge.

Or get to sleep early. I toodled around emailing contacts from the convention 'til about ten, then opened up the inbox on my email client. The avalanche of emails from Rachel started pouring in. Looked like she'd given up on text messages when I told her I was going on the road—probably didn't want to distract me when I was driving over the ice.

"This is Lantham 911, what's your emergency?" I muttered to myself as I opened the first one.

It read:

Situation escalating. Southland Corp. account, five stores. Inventory losses. Still no joy with earlier problem. Need to revive stakeout, not enough of me to go around. Need referral to separate agency. Advise ASAP.

Short, irritable, and to the point. She was at least dependable.

The second email:

Southland's getting squirrelly. Demand round-the-clock surv. or referral to subcontractor, or they threaten contract break. Someone over there is rattled. Got bead on a couple off-duty cops who could use the extra work.

The following emails were all updates—resumes and contact info for the off-duty cops. Looked like she managed to get it all together over the course of the day.

I dashed off a quick reply:

Rachael-

Car wreck and legal troubles have me stuck here 'til Tuesday—hoping for weather break Tues afternoon. Everything under control. Southland plan sounds good. Email forms so we can keep everything nice and legal. Phone charged, I'm in range, call if you need anything. Good work.

-Lantham

That killed about a half an hour.

I shut the computer and went to bed, tossed around for about an hour, then gave up and pulled the laptop back up to do a bit of mindless web-surfing.

Only another four hours until I hit my normal bed time.

1:00 AM, MONDAY

THE LITTLE PENDULUM CLOCK in my room dinged one with a little pixie chime. A few seconds later I heard some light footfalls in the hallway. Someone coming to my room by the sound of it. I clicked out of the porn site I wasn't interested in anyway—listlessness is the world's number one cure for eroticism, as any housewife will tell you.

Tap tap tap.

A light knock.

I closed the lid on my laptop and shrugged into a bath robe.

"Come in."

My niece, about four foot nine in her stocking feet, opened the door and slipped in. "Uncle Clarke?" Her voice was quavering, and she was shaking. It wasn't cold in the house—typical of people in cold climates, they kept it almost too warm for clothes in here.

"Yeah, honey, what's wrong?"

She looked left and right, like she was afraid the walls would hear, then gave me a pathetic helpless face.

There was a chaise next to the desk. I flipped my hand at it. "Have a seat. Tell me what's wrong."

This is probably not the most opportune time to point out that I'm not all that great with kids. My memories of being one don't seem to square up with how they react to things, or how their parents treat them like poorly-constructed Fabergé eggs. I do my best, and then do my best to get out of the situation ASAP.

She shuffled over to the seat, I settled down in the desk chair where I'd been a few moments before. Once she was sitting, she tried once or twice to speak, then she curled up in a ball in a corner. Terrified.

I leaned forward and gave her hair a little tousle. "Sarah, you came in here to tell me something. What is it?"

"The house," she whispered, "it's haunted."

"Haunted? Like with a ghost?"

"Yeah."

Poor kid was having nightmares, and she came to me rather than her parents. Odd. But then, one of her parents was my brother, who was about as warm and fuzzy as a crocodile. "Honey, ghosts can't hurt you. They're like dreams. They look scary, but as soon as the lights are on, they go away."

"No. They're here all the time."

"How do you mean?"

"I hear them in the walls. I see them when I go to the bathroom, out the window in the yard. Walking through the halls."

"Them?"

"Yeah."

"What do they do?"

"They...they..." She clammed up for a second, but her eyes were wide and didn't blink, staring past me into the middle-distance, "they whisper. And they walk, outside in the yard."

"You can hear them?"

"Every night."

"Now this is very important, Sarah. What do they whisper about?"

She hesitated, and then said a word with almost no breath behind it. "Daddy."

"What do they say about him?"

"They say he's in trouble. They say he's going to die."

If she was having dreams like this, it probably wasn't the greatest time to introduce this kid to the notion of universal mortality. "Why didn't you tell your parents?"

"Because the ghosts...they'll kidnap me if I do."

There's a wrinkle. Very lucid dreams. "What did they say, exactly?"

She made her voice grated and harsh like that kid from *The Shining*, "If she finds out, I'll take care of it."

Yup, should have stayed at the Airport Hilton. Dammit. "It's okay, sweetie, it's okay." I mimicked Samantha's soothing voice as best I could. "Nobody's gonna hurt you. Here, lie down. They won't know to look for you here."

I retrieved a spare pillow from my bed, and a blanket from the chest at the foot of it, then bundled her up on the chaise and, at her insistence, told her a story—trouble was the only one I had on tap with the weather outside was a Robert Service poem involving death, cremation, and communication from beyond the grave, none of which I realized until I was in the thick of it, so I found myself scrambling to play up the comic elements over the dark, and then finished it with a short moral. "Ghosts can't hurt you. Worst they can do is scare you, 'cause they only exist in your dreams. When you're sleepy your mind can make you hear things, and that's okay. It can't do anything bad to you, okay?"

She looked dubious. The fact that I was bullshitting as fast as my tongue could trip probably showed on my face, but it didn't seem fair to give her a lecture on proper critical thinking when she came to me for help in the middle of the night—particularly when something about her story had me chilled down to my slipper-socks for entirely different reasons.

"You're making that up."

I shrugged. "Okay, I'm making it up. I've never run into a ghost before."

"You're good at figuring things out, right?"

"That's my job."

"If I hired you, would you find the ghosts and make them go away?"

I made a show of considering it. "Do you have a quarter?"

"No." She dug around in the pockets of her PJ pants and produced a five spot, "All I got's this."

"Okay, you got yourself a detective." I stood and went to my overnight bag and got her four-seventy-five in change, then returned to squat next to the chaise. "Here's your change. I'm yours 'til Tuesday. If I don't find anything out, you'll get a full refund. Deal?"

She nodded her head sternly once, and took my proffered hand, shaking it with as much determination as a ten-year-old girl can manage (which is to say, more than most adults I'd run into). "Deal."

"Okay. You go to sleep. I'll keep my eyes out for ghosts."

She yawned, then settled down against her pillow. She mumbled "Okay," but only got halfway through before she was well and firmly in the grip of a new dream.

4:00 AM, MONDAY

FOUR CHIMES.

Other than the hourly sound of the chimes, and Sarah's soft breathing, and the periodic dull rumble of the furnace, there wasn't a lot of noise in the house. No computer fans reached me, no ambient chatter or street noise.

Eerie quiet. Like someone was watching. Breathing, but too quiet to hear. The hairs on the back of my neck stood straight out.

It was the kind of environment where four light chimes and a single creak were enough to roust me.

There. Another creak. It came on and tailed off slow and low rather than sharp—someone was spending a lot of time on each step, definitely not interested in being heard.

I slipped out of bed, pulled on my robe over the Kendo pants I'd worn to bed in deference to Sarah's presence, tucked my toes into the slipper-socks, and light-footed it to my door. On the way I grabbed my phone off the desk, out of habit more than anything.

Sarah didn't stir. The door was well-oiled—it hadn't squeaked the last few times anyone had been through it, and it didn't squeak now.

The hall, wide enough to be a living room in my corner of the world, had walls populated periodically by the kind of print-on-canvas reproductions of impressionist paintings that pretended to be genteel while screaming "conspicuous consumption" at volume eleven.

Okay, I know, class warfare is just disguised self-pity most of the time: about as sexy as watching a pig piss. You know what else is that sexy? Showy taste. I might have found the place inviting if it felt like something the people here loved, but I knew my brother well enough to know he didn't give two shits about any of this stuff beyond the thrill of people oohing and ahhing at the wealth on display.

Oh, well. I could hate my brother on my own time. I was on the clock now—I had a ghost to catch.

No one in the hall. The late-night prowler had already slipped into whatever room they were off to.

I stuck well on one side of the hall, on the assumption that the floorboards would be most worn and prone to creak under the throw rug that ran down the middle. The dark-stained hardwood floor wasn't cold, and in my socks it neither complained under my weight nor slapped back against my feet.

Two rooms along I ran into the first obstacle on what would prove to be quite the course. This was the kind of place where people kept their doors cracked open at night. Not a lot of hide-the-pickle going on in this corner of the world. Pity.

Peering into the crack in the first door, I didn't see anything but a lump in the bed. No way to tell who, but whoever it was snored just a little bit. Ragged, but steady, the kind of snore that's hard to fake—not that anyone here should be acting like a subject of one of my normal snoops, but you get mental habits in a job like mine that keep you alive. And alone, but that's another story.

I crept along—the next room was empty. Judging by the

state of the bed, whoever slept in there didn't sleep well. Probably the person I'd heard creaking earlier, by why the sneaking? It would help if I knew who slept where, but at four in the morning I wasn't likely to find anyone who could give me a map.

"...problem, okay?" Someone who sounded suspiciously like Sam raised their voice somewhere else in the house. It came more from in front of me than behind me, so I quickened my pace as best I could.

Garbles of another voice I didn't recognize filtered through to me. Maybe one coming through a speaker, followed by more of Sam's voice. I couldn't grab many words, but I knew that tone from days gone by: frantically protesting his innocence in the way that he only did when he was clearly guilty as hell.

I hung a right at the end of the hall and started down the stairs. Sam's voice reverberated up through the stairwell, close now, probably just off the annex at the bottom.

"No," he said, "We're good."

"If you're lying to me..." The voice was definitely coming from a speaker phone. Someone at his office? Maybe.

"I took care of everything."

"Everything?"

"Everything. Even if it goes south, we'll be covered. Now, do me a favor and get things..." The stairs under me creaked. Sam stopped mid-sentence. "Hold on a second."

The door to his study opened, the light threw his shadow out into the hallway. I froze, but I could see his feet from where I was. All he had to do was look up. I started mentally compiling a plausible story when he interrupted me: "Cynthia! You still here?"

The maid's voice came from almost right under me. "Mrs. Lantham asked me to stay over the holiday for the..."

"Right, right, fine. I'm on a business call. Get lost, will you?"

"Uh...sure." Rattled, hurried. She'd been eavesdropping too?

I heard some water run in a sink, then she hurried across my field of view and toward the dining room.

The door to Sam's office closed, Sam groused a little more to the voice on the other end of the line, then the door opened and clicked closed again. Heading off to bed at four thirty in the morning—and I thought I was a night owl.

Too bad his bedroom was somewhere in the hall behind me.

His foot hit the stairs at the bottom of the switchback well below me. I keyed up the biggest sleepy-faced yawn I'd used since the days when I used to beg off church on the grounds that I would snore during Mass.

"Clarke." He grumbled as we passed each other. Too wrapped up in his own anxiety to hassle me.

"Sam." I matched his greeting, chased it with a yawn, and finished my stumble down the stairs managing to appear more or less like I was looking for the bathroom but hadn't yet figured out what house I was in.

Turned out Sam had spotted Cynthia in a little water closet under the stairs. I ducked in and waited, counting Sam's retreating footfalls through the ceiling.

About halfway down, the steps stopped and a door closed. That would put him in the room with the tousled sheets—and no other people in the room, so he and Samantha weren't sharing a bed. Not exactly the day's most shocking news—in the few hours I'd spent talking with the family, I hadn't seen them so much as make eye contact.

For hallway ghost candidates, I had Sam, Cynthia, and parties unknown. Sam's bedroom was between me and my room, so he wouldn't have crossed my door on his way in. Cynthia would have had to negotiate the creaky stairs, but she was a light-framed woman who (I presumed) knew the house intimately, so she might have been able to slip down undetected.

It's niggling puzzles like this that get me standing in a bathroom in the house of relatives I don't like in the suburbs of a city I hate during a snowstorm on the night before Christmas. Wild geese and me, right?

Once I was sure Sam wasn't coming out again, I slunk across the hardwood and turned the office door handle. But I didn't turn it far. He'd locked the thing, dammit.

There was a goodly amount of light to see by—subdued, but enough to examine the lock. Looked like a garden-variety Schlage like you'd find at any home and garden center—pretty new, too. Judging by the lack of wear on the top of the handle and the lack of scratches around the keyhole, and assuming he used this room every day, it was less than a year old. Something recently upped his need for security.

Prurient interest. In the words of Rachael: I can haz.

Stupid Netspeak.

"Eh-hem."

I checked left to find Cynthia in a silk wrap and bunny slippers, leaning against the wall.

Like a kid caught spying on Santa Claus. I waited a beat for her to follow up the grunt. She didn't. She merely crossed her arms to emphasize her authority—but her eyes weren't as piqued as she wanted me to think she was.

"I...uh...a mosquito crawled in."

"Hmmm..."

The moment stretched for another short space of eternity. My lower back starts complaining if I squat or bend too much—hazards of living life too close to forty—so it was the ultimate arbiter of our standoff.

Besides, I didn't have my lock picks with me. I listened to my sciatica, and gave. "Got any hairpins?"

She pursed her lips and raised an eyebrow at me. "I've got tea."

"I suppose I could settle for..."

A scream shrill enough to scrape the brains off the inside of my skull raced through the house. I didn't realize I was running until I'd made it six steps down the hall.

I had a mental map of maybe ten percent of the house, and none of it was of this end, so I followed my ears. Toward the front of the house, past a jog in the hall, over ground I was going to have to retrace under non life-and-death circumstances, I found Samantha in the living room, pressed with her back against a wall, breathing fast and trying like hell to get herself under control. The aggressive fire in the fireplace and the insane pace of blinking Christmas tree lights lit the room like a bad carnival ride.

"Sam?" I thrust myself into her field of view and grabbed her shoulders. "Sam!"

She jolted, her focus shifted to me. Shock, relief, regret, the shadow of shared moments, and about six other emotions flickered across her face like pages in a flipbook before she seemed to remember herself. She took a breath, looked me in the eye, and said: "There."

A finger with guitar-string calluses stretched from under the cuff of her loose caftan-style shirt. The fact that she'd kept up with her axe lent me an uncomfortable sort of reassurance—good thing, too. At the other end of her sightline, a shattered bay window opening onto the front of the house let in the subzero night air.

No snow tonight. Just wind. And it was making my testicles crawl back up into my abdomen.

"What happened?" In a normal house, two strides would have taken me across the living room. Here it took six.

No glass on the ground. The window broke outward.

"I was watching the fire," she was stammering, but with my leg hairs growing inward to hide from the cold I figured it was more from the temperature than the fright, "and...you're gonna think I'm crazy, but I swear to God, he was in this room."

"Who?" I tossed it over my shoulder while I leaned over the broken glass and looked at the ground outside. Nothing but glass shards.

"I don't know?" I kid you not, I could *hear* the question mark.

"That was a question?"

"It...I don't know what it was. A man, maybe, but...God, you're gonna think I'm crazy, but he wasn't *here*."

"The ghost?" Cynthia's voice made me whip around. She was pulling a blanket from a basket-chest at the end of the sofa, taking it to Samantha.

"Ghost." And here I'd been under the impression that I'd already put the ten year-old to bed.

Samantha pulled the blanket tight around her shoulders and nodded. "Things have been happening. Little flashes in the corner of my eye. The kids have been having nightmares. I figured it was just holiday jitters, I mean, you know my parents...just..."

"How did the window break?"

"Oh. That." She hung her head a bit. "I...uh...threw a vase."

I took another gander at the dark ground outside the window. It all looked like glass to me, and the hole in the window was pretty damn impressive. It was an old house though, old enough that the glass in the mini-panes around the frame was warped and runny. A vase right through the middle could have shattered the whole center pane.

"Never let it be said that you take shit from anyone." I retreated from the window. "Let's get somewhere warmer. Cynthia, you said something about tea?"

"Yes. I'll get the kettle on." She disappeared from the room, back in functionary mode.

I moved to the door and checked the hall. Old cop programming—saved my life more than once. But in my brother's house, despite the fact that it *is* Sam we're talking about, it felt ridiculous. Or, it would have, if my hackles weren't crawling up the back of my neck like a centipede.

It wasn't the cold. There was something *wrong* in that room. I didn't know what it was, but every minute I stayed in there, I got surer that someone was about to step out of thin air and shiv me in the back.

I looked at Samantha and jerked my head into the hall. She stood and jogged out past me. I pulled the pocket doors shut across the doorway.

As soon as they were closed, the hackles started to relax. A little.

"Tell me about the ghost." I barked my order at the door. I didn't really want to talk to her—last thing this trip needed was more complications.

Samantha sucked her breath in, so loud I almost jumped. The hackles came back out to play, and this time they brought friends.

"There were always stories. They didn't say anything when we bought the house, but you hear things, you know? Like there was a murder here during Prohibition. Well, a lot of murders." She started walking, just a saunter, one foot in front of the other, like she was using charm school as a calming meditation.

"Hmph. Hauntings. You sure this isn't England?"

She laughed. Some very young part of me that never grew up still missed that laugh. "Oh, it's way worse. This is Seattle, realm of the enthusiastically morbid."

"You should make the brochures say that. You'd get a lot more tourists." We made the jog around the end of the hall. Now back on more familiar ground, heading toward Sam's office. "So, you bought a haunted house..."

"And it wasn't a problem. And then, a few weeks ago..." she trailed off, seemed to chew over her words for a few steps. "No, that's not fair. He's...it's not his fault."

"Sam?"

She nodded. "A little after school started, the kids all had nightmares. I didn't think...but now..."

"Nightmares?"

She sighed. "They all said they were hearing things. Then, seeing ghosts. I thought they were crazy 'til..."

"'Til you saw it, too. How long ago?"

"Halloween. When the first snow fell." Her arms, long since crossed over her chest, tightened, like she was trying to hug herself. "You know me. You remember I'm not superstitious, right?" She fingered the crystal at her collar bone.

"People change."

"No," she said, "They don't. They just stop being able to hide. When the frost came, at night the house got...creepy. Like there's always someone watching. Right in the corner of your eye. A shadow in the background."

"Like Peter Pan's scary cousin."

"Yeah. There were so many murders here, Clarke. So many. They brought informers here to kill them, and now it's like someone woke them up..."

"The ghost?" My brother's voice, behind us. When I turned to check, I noticed how close we were walking—if she hadn't been hugging herself, we'd have been holding hands.

Old habits'll bite you on the ass when you're not looking. More whipped cream on top of this peachy vacation, goddammit.

Sam stepped down from the stairwell across from his office. "It stalks the halls at night. It came from beyond the grave!" He raised his arms and shook them like a bogeyman from a B-movie.

Samantha said nothing. She didn't need to. Her posture said everything.

"You always could make anyone believe anything. Now, if you'll excuse me," he said, putting his hand on Samantha's shoulder, "We should be getting to bed before we wake any of the children. So should..."

My pocket interrupted with the most annoying part of the 1812 Overture. I chose that ring tone just for Rachael, who couldn't bring herself to phone unless there was some kind of the-world's-gonna-end emergency. "Sorry, bro, I gotta take this."

I pulled the phone out of my pocket, wandered down the hallway a few steps. After I'd checked to see that Gomez and Morticia had retreated up the stairs, I answered with all the put-upon yawniness I could muster on short notice.

"Rachael, it's butt-fuck-thirty in the morning."

"Cut it out, I know you don't sleep when you're not on a case."

"Fine. What's up?"

"Your pet primate is sleeping in the hallway outside the office."

"Come again?"

"I came in from the stakeout to offload my notes, and she's sleeping in front of the office door."

"She?" Pet primate? "You mean Nya Thales? From..."

"No, I mean Koko the Gorilla—of course it's Nya Thales."

"What the hell is she doing there?" I reached the end of ten paces, turned on heel, and headed back to the annex.

"She's been calling the office for two weeks."

Rachael was filtering my messages. Lovely. "You know that thing about you working for me?"

"So fire me when you get home."

"Fine. What's she want?"

"I don't know what she wants. Her phone messages kept asking for you."

"So why didn't you forward them…"

"Lantham, when someone throws poisoned meat at a dog, you don't let the dog get it."

"A dog." I drew even with the office door and squatted down. I plucked a hair off my head and licked it, then ran it over the seam between the door jamb and the door, below the handle.

"Duh. Conspiracy? People trying to kill you? Last thing you need is another woman in distress."

"Oh, trust me," I stole a peek at the empty staircase. "I've had my fill."

"Yeah, well anyway, you want I should tell her to get lost?"

"Have you found out what she wants yet?"

"Is she a customer? No, didn't think so."

"Maybe she wants to hire us. Find out what's up, and *email* me. I can't talk much here."

"Here? What's going…"

"I gotta go." I hung up and checked the clock on the phone's face. Four forty-five. Only a couple hours left 'til sun-up.

Good thing: after today, I was just about ready to call up my sanity and dump it like a ditzy girlfriend. For the sake of the well-being of the universe, the night needed to end before *another* Lantham wrote reality off like bad debt.

I'D FORGOTTEN ABOUT TEA, but Cynthia hadn't. The pot's whistle called me.

Despite being more of a coffee guy, the tea wasn't half bad. Neither was the company. Twenty seven and on her second masters, this one in journalism—studying to go into a job with even more dead ends than homicide, but that's the privilege of idealism—and she wasn't without her opinions, or stingy about them.

"...and your sister-in-law could do with a serious bonobo handshake."

I raised an eyebrow. "Bonobo handshake?"

"Well, your brother is a classic chimp type..."

"I thought you were a journalist."

"First masters in primatology. You learn a few things."

"Oh, I had no idea, please continue, Ms. Attenborough."

She favored me with a dip of her head, then went on in an affected high British accent. "Chimps are the politicians of the animal kingdom; highly canny posturers that take what they can get, because they never know what nature will provide. They build and protect their harems with violence, the males always insecure in their power, but they are not without their tender side..."

"Yup, you got him in one."

"Bonobos, their close cousins, take the opposite approach. For them, power issues are resolved with sex—a friendly genital rubbing or a bout of penis fencing is just their way of saying hi."

"Ah. Bonobo handshake."

"Yeah."

"So you don't live here, right? What are you doing here so late?"

I caught her in the middle of a sip, which provoked her

into some fairly elaborate hand waving before she could talk again. "I'm technically entitled to a room in the servants' quarters..."

"Servants' quarters?" A new level of decadence presents itself at Casa Lantham in Poseurville.

"Mm...everyone else lives back there."

"Everyone?"

"The butler, the chaffer..."

"Names?"

She laughed. "If you got into this job to get laid you got a long way to go."

"Oh, but I'm hanging on your every word. Chicks dig that, right? I'm just in it for the handshakes." I hid an incipient grin behind my mug.

She just about sprayed me with tea. "God, don't do that!"

"Goofy is what I got."

"Mm...in spades. So what's the deal with you and Sammy?"

"Sammy, not Mister Lantham?"

She rolled her eyes, "He's not here to piss off."

So, not familiar cause she thinks he's the bee's knees. "You like him too, eh?"

"Off the record?"

"Record? Until today I hadn't talked to him in longer than they've been married."

"He's the reason I don't live back there anymore, unless Mrs. Lantham wants me to help out with the kids for a weekend." No sneer or coldness when she mentioned Samantha. She'd picked sides.

"You're not a nanny."

"Nah, but they're good kids, and it's good practice."

"Hardly the best way to practice," I peaked my eyebrows in a bit of a flirt. We both broke down giggling. "Okay, okay, but seriously, I gotta know if he's still the same...um...prick?...that he was when we were kids."

"You mean does he try to be everyone's best friend, then get pissed and start shouting when he's not the most popular guy in the room?"

"So it wasn't just me."

"Hell no. I could never tell whether he was going to scream at me or tell me to rub his feet."

"So why do you stay? Hell, I'm his brother and he doesn't get that kind of loyalty."

"You really want to know?"

"Eh, maybe not. I just like asking questions."

She sighed. "Those kids need someone around who isn't nutty as a sack of squirrels."

That one made me smile—for real this time, not as part of the play. "Good job they've got you here."

"Even a crap job has a few perks. You tired yet?"

She'd caught me rubbing my eyes. "Yeah." I set the tea down and looked around the cavernous kitchen. Yup. Tired enough I couldn't tell which door I came in. "Where can a guy get a map of this place?"

"Come on," she set her mug down and took me by the arm, "I'll show you."

A little more flirting along the way, but nothing serious. Nothing useful either. The house was constructed like an old castle, four long halls around the edges, doors everywhere. She walked me up the south side of the house, where I hadn't been before. I left her at the stairwell, begging off on the grounds that there were people sleeping, and a Sarah in my room.

I stopped at the door to listen, make sure that Sarah was still breathing soft.

A little ways back up the hall, my eyes caught a painting lit by a little spot concealed in the ceiling. It showed the Bay, with the Golden Gate in the distance. A memory of home for Sam?

I'd only been gone a week. Just a week, and I don't think I've ever felt so homesick as I did for those couple minutes when I couldn't tear my eyes away from the mottled brush-strokes.

For some reason, it helped me sleep.

7:30 AM, MONDAY

INSOMNIA IS ONE OF THOSE SNEAKY THINGS—when you finally do get to that blissful oblivion, someone could smother you in your sleep and you wouldn't know a thing about it until you'd slipped right past bliss into just plain oblivion.

Fortunately for yours truly, the criminal attempting to smother me this morning prefaced her attack with a loud shriek of "It's CHRISTMAS! Uncle Clarke, wake up! Wake up!"

I defended myself valiantly with the strategic use of pillows. Even after she was joined by her two brothers, I escaped relatively unharmed.

Breakfast, presents. I retreated to my room to avoid church. The family decided to slum it, and walked down the hill to the bus stop for the Divine Word Mass—good old Lanthams, Irish Catholics to the core, even willing to make a show of poverty on a High Holy Day, just to appear extra penitent.

That wasn't really fair—when we were kids, Sam's favorite part of the Christmas tradition was riding the bus to Mass, because we couldn't afford the gas for non-essential trips.

Still, gave me a couple hours where I didn't have to worry

about playing nice with the hosts.

Did you know you can go crazy without vitamin D? I hadn't had what any sane person would call "sunlight" in a week now—not even sunlight filtered through a window. Hadn't seen the Bay either.

An attempt to take a quick tromp around the grounds for exercise netted me a twisted ankle when I stepped on an uncleared patch next to the south driveway and learned the meaning of the word "ice." Again. Water had some really stupid ideas about how to behave in this part of the world.

If memory served—and generally it doesn't, particularly not memories you've tried desperately to repress in an attempt to rid your mind of vast swaths of interminable boredom—the service should last at least an hour. Factor in travel time, I could maybe get a handle on some of the decidedly un-Lanthamy weirdness afoot in this ghastly pseudo-castle before they got back.

First stop, the outside of the window Samantha smashed last night. Someone—maybe Cynthia, maybe another one of the servants—had already swept the drive, but some glass still glinted from between the icicles in the planter. No footprints in the snow. No depressions in the flower-bed dirt that, due to its protection from the eaves, remained snow-free.

A good ten feet from the edge of the concrete to the window. Whoever she'd thrown the vase at had managed to cross that space without leaving tracks. Assuming there'd been anyone at all. Hysterics were looking mighty good as explanations go.

Assuming it wasn't just a ploy to get my attention. Memories of happier times—particularly with the after-the-fact editing that people in their thirties do when they realize that life isn't the constant parade of pleasure and glitz that their teenage selves expected—make people do boneheaded things.

I didn't know whether to be flattered or frightened. Then again, Kristine Warner aside, my taste in women seems to tend uncomfortably toward the psychotic.

The view from inside the window wasn't much different in terms of the facts, but the creep factor had me ready to jump through the roof. No scuffs in the carpet near the window, not that I should have expected any. Sitting where Samantha had said she was and watching the fire didn't show me anything. Yup, she had a straight shot out the now-covered-by-a-shutter window.

For reasons I couldn't put my finger on, I was certain someone was behind me. Even though my back was to the wall.

There wasn't a hidden spy-hole or door in the wall. I know. I checked.

Three times.

In my pocket, a cannon went off, followed by an insistent brass barrage. Rachael again.

"Clarke Lantham, plaything of fate."

"She wants to move in with me."

"Come again?"

"Nya. She's run away from home. She says you're the only person she trusts."

"And where do you come into the picture?"

"I'm her age, she thinks I'm cute, she knows I work for you. I'm an honorary tribe member."

"Lovely."

"Say that again? Your phone's buzzing."

"There's nothing wrong with my phone. Look, just give her a cookie and…"

"I'm not kidding, Lantham. You gotta do something about this Neanderthal."

"Very funny. What do you expect me to do from here?"

"I don't know. Call her. Tell her to go get a job. Anything."

I rubbed my face, hoping that somehow I'd wipe away one or two accreted layers of stupid from the day. "Look, I can't deal with this right now, okay? I'm in trouble up here..."

"What the..."

"Just shut up and listen, okay? Let her take my cot for a couple days, I'll deal with her when I get there. Do not let her interfere with the business, even if that means kicking her out in the morning and not letting her in again 'til after close. Let her use the fridge, I'll pay you for whatever."

"Your phone..."

"Fuck my phone. Just give her the room."

"What are you going to do when you get back?"

"I don't know. I don't want to think about it right now. Last time I saw her she just about died. Not a night I'm gasping to relive, okay?" I realized I was shouting. I didn't know when I'd started.

"Don't you talk to..."

"I'm sorry." I took a breath. "I don't know what's getting into me. Family stuff. Look, I really can't deal with this right now. I'll make it right after I get things here cleared up, and I'll bring you up to date on everything. Deal?"

"I want an asshole bonus."

"You'll get it."

"Deal." She hung up.

It was all I could do to keep from throwing the phone at the wall.

Pacing didn't help. Jumping jacks didn't help. My skin was crawling everywhere. The back of my mind started firing random images: Bodies. Murders. Hostages. Hunts. Like they'd all happened in this room.

There were ghosts in here—if I'd believed in them, I'd have been sure of it.

For the record, I don't believe in ghosts, but standing in that room damn near convinced me to change my mind. Something bad happened in there—I'd have laid even money that there had been at least two full-scale cannibalistic feasts and a handful of satanic rituals right where I was standing.

Just being in there made me want to call a priest.

I stalked out and slammed the door behind me. Paced back and forth, wandered the halls for a good five, maybe ten minutes. Somewhere in the underexplored parts I found a little atrium, open to the sky above. Might have been what the posh of the time would have called a "conservatory,"—working stiffs like me would call it a "greenhouse"—but somewhere along the line someone had knocked the ceiling out and put in French doors.

Like a snow-globe that hadn't been jiggled in a while. Some space to let my breath fog the windows 'til my breathing slowed down.

Nothing to learn in the living room. A check of my phone gave me about half an hour to do anything else that needed doing.

10:30 AM, MONDAY

A QUICK SQUINT AT THE DOOR showed the hair I'd stuck there last night hadn't been disturbed. Unless the office had another door, Sam hadn't had time to go in there yet. Coming back I'd taken the long way, and as far as I could tell I was alone in the house.

Christmas day, right? Good upper-class Catholic family? The help would go to their families after breakfast, or at least take the day off and hit a nice restaurant.

Me? I had some hair pins I pilfered from Samantha's bathroom cabinet. Not the easiest way to pick a Schlage, but it would do in a pinch.

I'd gotten half the pins when I heard a distinctive "eh-hem" from a yard to my left. I looked to the ceiling and shook my head.

"We've got to stop meeting like this," I said.

"You like doing things the hard way, don't you?" Cynthia's voice was followed by a jingle.

I gave up on the hairpins. "He'll fire you."

"You wouldn't tell on me, would you?" She hip-checked me out of the way and slid a key into a lock. "Your brother loses his keys a lot. He had Halifax—the butler—make a backup set."

The door swung inward.

I had to admit, when it came to decorating an office, my brother—or at least whoever he was trying to impress—had taste. Walnut shelves, lots of books. If he'd actually read half of them, there was one way in which he was a better man than I was.

That was fine. Every kid brother should have at least one thing he loved that his big brother didn't cast a shadow across.

I waved to Cynthia to stay outside, and took a minute to assess the space and remember what he'd said last night that spiked my nosy-bastard-o-meter.

I took care of everything. That was what he said. Classic cover-up stuff.

Trouble. Big trouble. And if I was going to help him—which I figured I owed him for bailing me out—I had to know what was up.

"Cynthia?" I waved her in and pointed to the phone on the desk, "This looks like the kind of thing you'd have in a big office. Does the house have its own PBX?"

"Its what?"

"A phone switch, handling multiple lines. Maybe a server room?"

She scrunched her face and scratched behind her ear. "I don't remember ever seeing one."

"Is there an IT guy that comes in to service things?"

She shook her head. "I don't think so. It's not really my thing."

The phone wasn't much more helpful. It had a caller ID memory, but I didn't see anything in the incoming calls for the last three days. Times like this, I wish I had Earl Whitaker on permanent retainer—he could tell me how to turn this thing into a remote-controlled flying dildo in five seconds using chewing gum and duct tape. This job was a twenty-five cent family special, though—no expense account.

"Is this the same phone you've got back in the kitchen?"

"Yeah, I think so." She shouldered me out of the way. "Looks the same. Why?"

"Not sure." I punched a couple more buttons—software buttons, poorly labeled. "Just wondering where...ah." One of them brought up the last ten numbers dialed. The most recent from last night.

Sam's tastes were baroque enough that he kept a fancy desk set, very little used, to the right of the phone. I carefully removed the top sheet of paper—didn't want to leave any ragged edges to tell the tale—and took a pen from its holder, scrawled the number down. I folded it and put it in my pocket.

The computer was still on, but a jiggle of the mouse told me he had it locked down—it would take a little work to get at what was inside. Assuming it turned out to be important—I really didn't want to have to wade through Sam's dirty laundry if I could help it. If nothing else, I'd have to be able to look him in the eye some day, when our mother died. Easier to do if I wasn't current on the particular rank of prickhood he'd managed to attain.

Still, it never hurts to get some insurance. "Mind if I keep those keys for the rest of the day?"

She grunted, like I was insane for even asking. Leaning against the bookshelf with her arms crossed and her lips pursed. Clearly waiting for me to make an offer.

"How 'bout I buy you dinner?"

"As in, I won't have to cook it?"

"As in."

"Tonight?"

"Sure."

She tossed me the keys. "Kitchen. Nine?"

Up to my room. Log in. About fifteen minutes before I entered the danger window for discovery. Granted, the worst that could happen was that I'd piss off Sam and we'd wind up rehashing every grudge he was still holding—the man could have filled all the books in his office with them—but I didn't really want to re-tread ground that was still locked in permafrost.

The plus of travel in the Internet age: I could carry most of my normal bag of tricks with me. I dropped the number into all three of my reverse-lookup services. All three of them dead-ended at the same T1 line. An investment bank in New York. That would take a bit of drilling down.

Much as I didn't want to admit it, I was still feeling a bit stir-crazy from earlier—and stupid. Losing it like that on the phone with Rachael. They didn't make profanity that was up to the job of describing that kind of dunce-headed assholery.

Now that the adrenaline was tailing off, a hidey-hole would have suited me just fine. Hell of a Christmas present to give her. Yeah, I know Rachael does her Christmas on the twenty-seventh with her family in Los Gatos, but it didn't change my programming.

I rapped my head against the wall a few times for good measure. Antsy from not enough time on the job? Angry because I'd rather be dealing with the small scale office drama than a trumped-up charge and a stint with family members I'd have been perfectly happy not seeing again for fifty years? Maybe.

As excuses go, it was thinner than the cheap toilet paper you find at truck stops. For self-respect, it did even less.

11:30 AM, MONDAY

SOMETIMES, EVEN WHEN YOU HAVE WORK TO DO, you have to break for a walk. I took a piece to get reacquainted with the front yard. Managed to resist the impulse to spell out "Fuck Seattle" with my footprints on the lawn.

The estate sat on a hill. A driveway swooped up from one gate to another that, from the air, would have looked like a circle with a bite taken out of one side. Two garages—the large one on the south side at the top of a cliff, and a smaller one on the north side—lolled straight driveways like tongues down to the curves of the "C."

As prisons go, it was the less rape-prone of the ones I'd been in this weekend—about the only thing going for it. That, and the sun was out, for all the damn good it did. Raised the temperature back up to almost thirty degrees—glinted off the roof and the lawn like someone turned on the sparklers.

God—whatever he wants to call himself—is a hell of a tease.

The north side of the property fell away down the side of a gentle slope, but only a few feet off the drive to the south, a hedgerow blocked the view into a forest that looked like it had been planted to stop the neighbors from peeping. Behind it, an ugly gully choked with brambles and dead-fall, except for a little playground directly below the bend in the driveway. Someone—hired help, probably; Sam wasn't one for finishing projects he started for reasons other than social mobility—had built a proper, old-style wood-and-metal fortress with swings, slides, and the whole shebang. The kind of place Sam and I used to defend with water balloons in the summer at the public park, trying to hold the high ground.

I moseyed down the path, staying mobile enough that my toes wouldn't turn black. The main perk of this job is that, even though most of your time gets eaten by termites—insurance verifications, background checks, adultery snooping—sometimes, just sometimes, you get to play Mighty Mouse. It might not do a hell of a lot in the grand scheme of things, but in a world filled with war and genocide and Disney On Ice, you do what you can. Me? I'd have killed for a bit of global warming.

Mighty Mouse, yeah. He gets to save the day, doesn't have to give a damn about the people. All the benefits of being a hero, none of the bother. When it's someone you don't know, someone who's hired you, you can swoop in and turn their life upside down. You can deploy your clue-by-four and have a fucking opinion, because the only thing you need from them is your check.

With family, it's different. Everything that makes you a good hired gun makes you a shitty intimate. Seen it on the force, seen it on the street, seen it across the pillow on the off-chance that there's something on the other side of it besides a blank wall.

Down here in the shadows, it was colder. But it was the first place since my car seduced the 4x4 that I didn't feel like someone was watching me.

"I owe you an apology."

I jumped, whirled around, unconsciously clutched at the small of my back for a gun that wasn't there—only Samantha's father. "Tom. What the hell..." I squeezed a little extra oxygen out of the frozen stuff they called "air" in this part of the world, "don't sneak up on me like that. It's not safe."

The look he gave me told me that he didn't need any further convincing. "Like...like I said. I owe you an apology."

"Yeah, you do." I wasn't in the mood to be gracious.

"Well, for what it's worth...I'm sorry. If I'd known..."

"Forget it. I did."

He pursed his lips, shook his head slowly, then turned away and started walking back up the hill. A few yards up the trail he stopped. "I saw another man do that once, you know. Reach for his gun whenever someone walked up. A part of him never got out of Vietnam, 'til eventually he couldn't stand to be anywhere else. Wouldn't talk to anyone about it. They found him in full dress, with his service weapon."

As he spoke, a breeze came down the gully and ran its fingers up my neck, but I just said "I'm fine. Thanks."

Family. Yeah. They were almost my family once. That would've been worse.

I climbed onto the kids' fort, situated myself in the top tier, and leaned onto the rampart that, when I knelt, was only slightly too tall for me. The inside was packed tight with snow, but it cleared easily. No ice—it hadn't gotten warm enough down here to thaw, then freeze again.

My brain tends to catalog the world that way when it's trying to avoid things. Makes it hard to get too bored.

Not sure how long I stayed down there. Long enough for my knees to go numb. Maybe longer. Down there, I didn't have to pursue the lookup—figure out who Sam had been on the phone with. I liked it better that way.

Back in high school, watching Sam trying to get girls to

climb into the back seat, was a bit like watching a dolphin do macramé. That was entertainment of a sort. Not so much when he started getting into trouble at work. When he got a taste for having people look up to him. When he turned the charm he was born with toward making people he found useful feel like they were struck from gold.

Problem was, when you're that slimy, that slick, you have to have a strong stomach. Sam never did. He could never lie unless he was convinced first. From the time he tried to cover up for his priest's infatuation with the other altar boys, to the cheating racket with his favorite history teacher, he kept getting himself in situations bordering on perjury. Wound up looking like an idiot, or worse. Always surprised when suddenly he didn't have friends anymore, again.

You can't play the social climbing game if you can't look your boss straight in the eye and lie through your teeth, and that's just for starters. He wouldn't have known truth if it cut his fingers off, but I'd never known him to pick a lie he could stick to long enough for it to do him any good. All guile, and no guts was my kid brother.

Doesn't take long for that kind of person to go sour. By the time I was twenty-four, he'd already tried to kill me once.

Once was enough.

"Clarke?" Samantha, the occasion for said fondly-remembered fistfight. She'd managed to make it all the way down the trail and sit on one of the swings, and I hadn't noticed.

You're slipping, Lantham.

"I came down here to be alone."

She stared into the middle distance ahead of herself—didn't react directly to me. "The kids are asking for you."

"Oh." Well, nieces and nephews didn't deserve to get in

the crossfire between the rest of their family—none of it was their fault. I pulled myself up to something that most independent observers would count as "standing," though with the feeling in my lower legs gone I wasn't convinced. It was enough to toddle over to the slide.

I wooshed to the pile of snow at the bottom. You've heard of freezing your ass off? It felt like my ass dropped off my body the second I planted it on the cold metal.

Standing, dusting myself off before the powder melted and got me wet. "Any idea what they want?"

"Laser tag. We got them a couple sets for Christmas. Jimmy's convinced his Uncle is a crack shot."

A childish grin tugged at parts of my face that hadn't gotten a lot of practice in the last day-and-a-half. "Sounds like fun. Thanks." Without thinking about it, I dragged my fingers across her shoulder as I walked past.

Old habits. Bad habits.

She caught my hand before I was out of reach, but she didn't look up at me. "They should have been yours."

Not pleading. She'd grown up more than that. Just a flat statement, what she took to be a fact.

I didn't look down at her. I didn't shout. I didn't even bother with an edge in my voice. I just took my hand back. "If you ever say that again, I'll tell Sam why you married him."

12:30 PM, MONDAY

"OKAY," I STRAPPED ON MY chest sensor, "You guys know how this works, right?"

"We played at the one in Reno. I totally kicked their ass." Albert did a victory dance.

Sarah stuck her tongue out at him. Jimmy—silent, determined, already playing out his revenge in his head—just gripped his gun barrel with his grubby left hand and fingered the trigger with his right. It was only a plastic gun, true, but a part of me winced to see the oily handprints he was leaving all over it. Probably hadn't washed up from lunch.

"So, you wanted to play with me, I've got a few special rules."

"Special rules?" Albert, not entirely thrilled with the idea.

I ran them through basic safety.

"But," Jimmy said, "These aren't real guns."

"You treat them like they're real, or we don't play."

"Why?"

I looked him straight in the eye, "Because I've killed people, and I've seen people die because they didn't respect their weapons. This is a game, and you don't want me to forget it's a game. Trust me on that one." The two boys blanched.

Now that I had their attention, "So, you keep the gun pointed at the ground until you're ready to aim at someone. You don't point it at anyone or anything who's not playing. You keep your finger off the trigger until you're ready to fire. Deal?"

They all nodded, like they weren't sure they still wanted to play.

"All right," I smiled and held my weapon at low-ready, "let's rock and roll." I switched it on. "You guys ready?"

Seeing my smile, they were okay again.

"Everyone count to fifty," said Albert, "Then start!"

We broke. Everyone ran for cover.

Those kids gave me a run for my money. Energy that would make any speed freak hang his head in shame. We were technically playing every man (or kid) for himself, but they quickly figured out that I was the biggest threat. Unite around a common enemy? It's programmed into our DNA, and they fell into it quick. The game was to fifteen points. I'd pick one off, another kept coming. Whooping, hollering, cheering like only kids who've completely forgotten themselves can do.

Albert was the pack alpha. That kept him out in front, taking the most hits. By the time they backed me into the fortress, he only had one hit left.

On my retreat up the slide, they pegged my back sensor. I used my three-second reset to duck below the rampart. Sarah scrambled up behind me. I rolled and fired, hitting her chest sensor as soon as she crested the top of the slide.

"Better go down."

"Nuh-uh."

"Two, one." I squeezed again, she took another hit.

"Hey, no fair!"

"You gotta use the reset to hide. Two…"

She dove down the slide, wound up head first in the pile of snow at the end.

I popped over the edge, weapon at the ready, aiming for Jimmy at the swing set.

He'd moved.

I dropped back down, put my back to the rampart, and listened. Under Sarah's spluttering, I heard the *crunch crunch crunch* of small feet on snow, creeping around to my right. I popped up over the edge and fired down on him from the top. Head shot.

And it gave Sarah the opening she needed to tag me from behind again. Good instincts, these kids. One point left for me. Two for Sarah. Two for Jimmy.

"Ooh, you guys are in trouble!" I said.

My sensor cleared. I popped up and tagged Sarah, dropped, rolled, popped up to get Jimmy—he'd moved on again. Smart kid.

Motion to my left. I fell back, thinking too late that I might crush my back sensor, and fired left. Bingo. His sensor flashed.

One more second, and Sarah would be vulnerable again.

Crunch crunch crunch crunch. Running light steps. She'd gone to ground. They were going to force me into the open.

"Fourteen all! Next shots win!"

I gave him about five seconds before...

Bam. "Hey!" Jimmy was down. I peeked over the edge, checked his eyeline, and followed it straight to Sarah.

Draw a bead. Squeeze. "Bang bang!"

The sensor on her chest squeaked and buzzed. Sarah's face went from triumphant to flummoxed in the space of two blinks. "Hey, no fair!"

"Oh, it's very fair. Albert?"

He'd been sitting on the swing set, watching the game. "Yeah?"

"Up for a different game?"

"Sure." He shrugged, a bit deflated from before.

I took another trip down the slide. "Okay, so, you guys all did good."

"We lost," Sarah wasn't having any of the reassurance pep talk.

"Yeah, but I've been doing this a lot longer."

"That's not fair," Jimmy said.

"No, it's not, but sometimes you gotta fight when the odds are against you. Do any of you know what your mistake was?"

None of them seemed to have any idea.

"You forgot who was most dangerous."

"How's that work?" Albert leaned forward. He smelled a chance for secret knowledge.

"You were all playing against each other, not just me. You know I'm the one who's got the edge to win, you should have taken me out first. Then played with each other."

"That doesn't sound like much fun," Sarah crossed her arms over her chest and kicked at the ground.

I shrugged. This really wasn't tactical training, and I didn't want to ruin their fun.

"Okay, then, new game. Teams. Me and Sarah, and you boys. We work together, you work together. See if that changes the odds."

Sarah bounced. The boys shared one of those telepathic looks that twins sometimes do.

"You're on!" They said it like they were both speakers rigged up to a common stereo.

Two on two. We went at it for two more rounds—they liked the new game so much that we never upgraded to capture the flag. By the end of the second they'd run me ragged as three-year-old blue jeans.

You know that thing where a two year-old will make you read *Green Eggs and Ham* until your brain turns to mush? These kids were like that with laser tag, and by the start of round three my knees went to jelly any time I wasn't running or crouching.

"Hey!" Sam, standing on the front porch, clapped hard. The slap-back echo from the house punched like a gunshot on each smack. "Time to go wash up for dinner." His words said "father." His tone said "bully." He was pissed off about something.

The kids, like members of a carsick choir, kvetched all the way up into the house. I followed. Game over, no reason to hang around in the cold with all this gear strapped to my carcass.

Sarah ducked through the door in front of me, but Sam held up his hand after she passed. "Not you."

He reached in and pulled the door closed. Squared his shoulders. Tried to stare me down. Even with two inches on me, he couldn't hold the stare for more than a couple seconds.

"There's probably something we should talk about."

"Oh?" I unstrapped the chest/back sensor belt. "Did I leave my socks in the bathroom?"

He jutted his chin out at the lawn. "Walk?"

I shrugged. "Sure." I piled my gear just off to the side of the front door where nobody would step on it. We then strode our fashionable way out on to the lawn, my brother and I. The only time we'd been in lock-step since we hit puberty.

It took him a good minute to work up the gumption to extort any more words from the English language. "I don't think it's a good idea to teach kids about guns."

"Then why'd you buy them the laser tag set?"

"Those aren't guns."

"Tell that to a cop who makes that mistake in the dark."

"God, you're a cynical asshole."

"Thanks. I work hard at it. Got a little trophy that I polish every day."

"I don't want you playing with them anymore."

"Fine with me, but you'll have to tell them why."

"No, I won't. I'm their father."

"Ha! That'll carry a lot of weight."

He grumbled, ground his teeth, and tried again. "It's my house. A bit of respect..."

"Look, bro, you don't want me to play with them, I won't play with them, but I'm not going to lie to them to make you look good."

"Just...Jesus, can't you just stop being an asshole for three seconds?"

"Nope. Too full of shit. I'd explode. Tell me what your real problem is, maybe we can make a deal."

"My real...why you..." he stopped in his tracks, pumped his fists open and shut like he was a blow-up doll trying to inflate himself to a more impressive stature. All it got him was a red face and a hell of a scowl. "Get out of my house."

"Happy to. Where do you want me to go?"

"What?"

"You posted my bail. You're legally responsible for me. I have to let you know where..."

"Go to hell."

"Better heating system anyway."

"What the..."

"Want to try again? Come on, Sam, tell me what you're pissed about. I'll fix it if I can."

"You want to know? You want to *know*! As if you didn't already know!"

"Spell it out for me, I left my brains in my other pants."

"Bet you fucking did." Well, at least he'd learned to swear semi-competently since I'd last seen him. "You come in here and start acting like you own the place, telling my kids what to do like you're the Dad in the house. Well let me tell you something, *bro*, you're nothing. You blew your chance to have this family. She picked me. She loved me, not you, okay? You can stop trying to steal it back, 'cause it was never yours in the first place. You're a sad little screw-up who couldn't keep his hands on the best thing that ever happened to him, and you'll never amount to a goddamn thing. And you're not going to wreck my family because I was enough of an idiot to bail you out of jail. You're lucky I let you lick the mud off my shoe."

I chuckled—I swear, it was the most diplomatic thing I could do. I was sitting on a full-on laugh volcano. "God, that must've felt good."

"What?"

"That rant. You've been waiting years to do that, haven't you?"

"I...uh..."

"Feels really good right now, with all the legal trouble?"

"The...uh...what?!"

Bingo. "Hard to be a banker these days. All that oversight. All that paperwork. Leverage is a killer, isn't it?"

The rage drained out of his face, just for a second.

"She's probably threatened to leave you," Twinge. "so that you don't drag the whole family down when you get fired?" No twinge. "Or when the indictments come down?" Twinge. "But nah, you wouldn't have told her about those, gotta protect the little woman." His face flushed again. "She's just tired of your shit—hiding in your office, yelling at the kids, barking at the servants...hitting on the maid."

"You son of a bitch!" He threw a right hook at my face. I faded with it, it glanced off my cheek, and followed it with my left straight up into his diaphragm.

The wind rushed out of him. He crumpled against me with a barely-audible whimper.

I wrapped him up in a bear hug. "Listen good, 'cause I'm

only going to tell you this once. I didn't want Samantha then. I don't want her now."

"Bu...bu...bullshit. You were engaged..." He started squirming. I gripped tighter.

"Oh, we wanted to get married all right. But Tom wouldn't let her hitch up with someone from our side of the tracks. He told her he'd cut her and the boys off from the money and out of the will."

Sam scrambled, got his feet under him and started wrenching free. I let him.

"Bullshit!" Oh, yeah. He had all his breath back now. Even the neighbors could tell.

"She proposed to me on the condition that I give up law enforcement and went into banking to get Tom's approval."

"Liar!"

"I turned her down."

"Shut up shut up shut up shut up!" He ran at me. I stepped aside. He went sprawling face first into the snow.

His technique wasn't bad, but I'd done this before. Too recently.

The last thing you want to do in a fight is reflect on what a hapless nincompoop your kid brother is. Gives him the chance to kick your shins out from under you.

And let me tell you, snow might be a culinary delight with cherry syrup on a summer day, but it sure as hell ain't all it's cracked up to be when you have to eat a mouthful of it at high speed.

He yanked my left shoulder and flipped me over. My face started complaining about all the fists hitting it. "Take it back you shit!" *Bam.* "She loves me!" *Thud.* "Not you! She loves me!" He started shaking me. "Get it through your thick skull. She'll never be yours. Never. You hear me, dickwad?" Somewhere, through the pain, I wondered about the mechanics of wadding up a dick. "You hear me?"

"Stop!" Samantha's voice, shrill. Off to the right.

"Do you? Answer me!"

I didn't have much in the way of brains or thoughts to spare, but I had a shitload of adrenaline, so I answered him the only way I could.

Fist, meet Sam's nose. Nose, say hi.

Sam's weight flopped off me, and I heard him whimpering next to me like a kicked dog.

Adrenaline. It's a beautiful thing. If they ever start selling it on the street, I'm gonna set myself up as a dealer. It lets you do things like stagger to your feet after you've had your face beaten in by a vindictive banker.

It gives you the presence of mind to appreciate how silly said banker looks plowing through the snow like a bulldozer, hoping it'll make his nose stop stinging.

It keeps you from falling over when a crowd of onlookers hits you like a football team.

And it helps you figure out that the voice comforting you is the one you least want in the world, and shrug her away like you do this every day. "See to your husband," I grunted, then started stalking my unsteady way up the hill to the house.

As you might expect on a High Holy Day, an unholy row erupted behind me. I turned in time to see Tom and Cynthia trying to keep Sam from attacking Samantha, who had sprawled back in the snow like she'd been pushed. After one or two feints in her direction, he turned and barreled up the hill toward me. I ducked out of the way as best I could—he continued past, into the house.

Where the hell is he going?

My instinct said "run after him." That look in his eyes wasn't quite murder, but it was close, and the kids were in there. But if I did, chances were my presence would push him over whatever edge he was dancing on.

"Tom!" I didn't bother with niceties. "Get in there and make sure he doesn't do anything stupid."

To his credit, Tom snapped to and hot-footed it up into the house.

Cynthia helped Samantha to her feet, and they both began the march houseward, leaning on one another like sisters. I shrugged and continued on my way.

Just as I mounted the first couple steps to the door, I heard a scream from inside the house. Face throbbing, I launched forward, reached for the door, and fell sprawling into the house as it opened in front of me.

Edith ran out past me shouting "No! Somebody stop him, please!"

No sooner was she past me than I heard the roar of a muscle car. I turned over and got to my knees in time to see a ragtop Aston Martin DB9 rip down the south side driveway at thirty miles an hour and accelerating. When he got to the sharp bend in the drive, he shifted into third.

The car didn't continue forward. When I heard the clutch drop, a light shone against the car, like lightning had struck a few feet away and the car's cherry-red finish was picking up the glow. And I swear, in that eye-blink instant, I saw a shadow cast across the lawn in that bright halo of light. The outline of a gangster in a hat, dull in the midday glimmer, but unmistakable.

The car slid left off the drive, as if the shadow had given it a friendly nudge.

It kept sliding.

Samantha screamed as it plunged through the hedge row at the crest of the gully right above the kid's playground.

She kept screaming as the car tripped on the granite block edging at the top of the cliff, and its left wheels buckled.

As I found my feet and started to run, the Aston enjoyed

its last few seconds as anything that could be properly considered a "car."

It flipped sideways, over the cliff, slamming top-first into the gully below.

You get used to adrenaline. You can get addicted to the way it blocks out pain.

And, when I got to the top of the trail, the way it blocks out nausea.

The Aston's last social encounter was with the top-level ramparts of the kid's faux-fortress. Even from the top of a hill maybe fifteen yards away, I could see the dark trickle starting down the slide.

I turned around and body-blocked Samantha, only a few steps behind me.

Cynthia arrived a second later. "You," I pointed at her, "Keep the kids in the house."

"But I..."

"Now!" She skedaddled.

"Let me go let me go I have to save him let me go," Samantha's mouth was going at least a hundred miles an hour faster than her brain. I took her face in my hands.

"Shh. Shh. Stop it! He's gone."

"No!"

That's the other side of adrenaline. It makes everyone else inhumanly strong too.

I kept my blood up enough to walk Samantha back from the edge, keeping myself between her and any potential eyeline, despite the way her fingernails kept insisting that she *needed* to get down there.

1:00 PM, MONDAY

First it was the fire truck.

Then it was the coroner.

Then it was the cops.

I managed to use the professional courtesy lever to get a look at the car before they trucked it away. I didn't have a burning desire to see what was left of Sam, but they were kind enough to package him up and cart him away to the land of the filing-cabinet refrigerators before they let me down there.

They set it on the flat-bed top-down—guess they didn't bring the equipment to flip it right-way up. There wasn't a hell of a lot to learn from it. The impacts had ruptured all the fluid lines, the thing was still dripping oil and coolant and brake fluid and gasoline and god-knew-what-else all over the place.

Well, actually, I knew what else. It smelled like hot metal and Ivory soap, and those are two smells you never forget. I just didn't want to think about it.

I wanted a shower. It would sting like hell—my face was already starting to beat at the front of my head in time with my pulse—but at that minute I'd have killed for a Brillo pad scrubdown all the same.

Always felt that way when I found a body. Doubly so, since

I damn well near killed this one for the stupidest reason next to a drug fix.

Goddammit, Lantham, when are you gonna learn to keep your trap shut?

I needed to get inside anyway, soon as possible. The adrenaline in my system was dumping out, meaning I'd collapse soon unless I could work up a good rage again. More important, it meant I had maybe half an hour, maybe less, before I had to completely disappear off Samantha's radar, and for the rest of the day, too.

Why? I'm gonna take a wild guess that most of you reading this have never seen someone killed. You've never had to shoot anyone, and you've never been on the other end of a gun or had life flash from benign and enjoyable to deadly dangerous and back again in the space of a couple minutes.

Lucky you.

You hear about the fight or flight response in grade school. They don't ever teach you about it again. They figure you've got the basics, which is nice, except it's crap. Because there is no fight or flight response.

But there is a fight, flight or fuck response.

Don't believe me? Ask any friend who's seen combat and who isn't too embarrassed at how they turned into slavering, prowling sex maniacs afterwards. It's the secret we've all got—it used to be part of the male code: We figured that scoring while deployed, or while on the beat, didn't count. Besides, women wouldn't understand if they found out, right?

Right. I got my education the first time I was partnered with a woman in a patrol car. Like with sex, adrenaline is a slow burn on women—slow to build, impossible to stop once it hits peak, sour at the tail end. For a man, it goes on and off like a switch. You go to a bar after to find a date, and if you can't you just joke about blowing your friends. If you're stuck in a war zone, that's exactly what you do, and nobody talks about it.

Adrenaline dumps do crazy things—and me and that partner did those crazy things all over the side of the road after our first shootout. We weren't the first. We weren't the last. But I learned that if you don't want your carrot waxed or your eyes clawed out, you steer clear of a woman after there's been a killing. Half an hour after you come down, she comes down. I didn't have a lot of time.

The truck pulled out of the driveway. I made sure the grandparents had custody of the kids. I told Cynthia to call someone to keep Samantha company and catch her when she finally hit meltdown.

Me? I needed a shower before I hit meltdown myself.

"ARE YOU OKAY?" CYNTHIA emerged from one of the bedrooms with a bundle of dirty linens in time to nearly collide with me on the way to the restroom.

"Peachy." I nodded at the bathroom door. "It free?"

"Yeah."

"Towels?"

"I'll bring some in."

"Fine. Thanks." I kept my eyes off hers. I've got a ritual for times like this, when I really need it. It's one thing to go into action, to have to do the whole bit with the cops, to have several hours to come down. It rattles you, but there's a procedure, and the procedure brings you down easy. But this was personal, and there was no procedure to make it all right again.

I was on my own, and I knew if I looked at her I'd haul her in with me for a—what did she call it?—bonobo handshake. She was as frivolous as I prefer, but I was miles from trusting my own judgment, and the last thing I needed was a complication.

Simple ritual:

Turn on the shower, heavy on the hot. Shuck the clothes, throw them on the toilet seat in something resembling a stack. Step through glass door into ostentatious marble shower stall. Shut door. Step under stream, raise face to water. Attempt not to scream when water hot enough to boil a clam hits you on the swollen, bruised, cut-to-shit flesh you earned courtesy your dead brother's rage fit. Which you provoked. Which drove him to his suicide.

Try not to bash your head against the wall to clear the conviction that you killed your brother just because he was a bastard. Killed him just as sure as if you put a gun to his head.

Take a breath. Clear your head.

Shampoo first.

Scrub.

Knead.

Get out all the panic-scented sweat. All the grime. All the guilt. All the rage.

All the blood.

Good.

Now, soap.

Take the soap.

Scrub the chest...

I dropped the soap and just about threw up. I scrubbed and rubbed in a blind panic trying to get it off me. I must have howled. Trying to get away. I slipped on the soap and barely caught myself on the grab bar and scooted back into the corner.

I wrung my hands, pushing pushing pushing trying to get that god-awful smell away.

"Clarke!" Cynthia tore the door open and jumped into the shower, trying to push me up.

Get away get away get that fucking thing away. I batted her hands away. "Get off!"

She started. In the little room my shout must've sounded like a bomb.

She slapped me, hard. Somewhere in the universe, a half dozen galaxies picked that moment to explode. "Clarke! Tell me what's wrong."

It was the right move. I got enough of my sense back.

"Soap. Get it out of here. Now. Please."

"Soap, got it."

She backed off, got the bar of Ivory, took it out of the shower.

The smell was still all over me. Like guilt. That's what it smells like. Ivory soap.

"Get me something else?"

"I've got some tangerine hand soap."

"That'll work." I set my jaw and pulled myself together. One foot under, one hand on the little marble seat.

I pulled myself to my feet. Reached out to the door and took the soap from her. I scrubbed my hands and chest until my skin went raw, then I doused my whole body, every nook and cranny, in the new, benign smell.

Finish the ritual. Get a good clean rinse. Face still throbbing, but that would heal.

When I got out of the shower, she was still there, with a towel about twice as long as I am tall. I accepted it and toweled it off.

"You okay?"

"Yeah." Believe it or not, I wasn't lying. "All systems functioning within normal parameters." Like Data from *Star Trek*.

She jerked her head at the window sill, where the soap sat. "What's the deal?"

"Oh, that." I finished drying the less dignified parts of my anatomy and wrapped the towel around me. "It's pretty gruesome."

"Ha." She sat down on the toilet, still soaked to the skin, and crossed one leg over another. "That's the whole day, it's not like one more thing is gonna hurt."

"You asked for it." I checked my hair in the mirror. Nothing new gone gray, nothing falling out yet. "You're not gonna believe it though. Ivory soap. Human brains smell like Ivory soap. Just one of those stupid things."

"Ew."

"Yeah. On a good day I can use the stuff, when it's all there is. Today...well, let's say I got too close to the car."

"Double ew."

"You should go get changed." I pointed to her soaked uniform. "You're gonna freeze in that getup."

"Mm...good point." She made to leave.

When she reached the door I said: "Thanks for the help."

"Don't mention it. You sure you're okay?"

"Yeah, I'm fine."

And I was. Really.

Head clear, check...

Anxiety scrubbed off, check.

Peace made with the dead? Not nearly.

By the time they drove off, the cops were already talking suicide—maybe accident. That didn't square with what I saw. Cars don't jump off the road like that without a good reason, and no precision driver on Earth can violate the laws of physics.

Problem was, I had seen a *shadow* appear next to the car, just for an instant, before it went haywire. Like the shadow had pushed the car.

A ghost?

If ghosts can push cars, then I need a different line of

work. Besides, I'd just had my face beaten in and I was mad as hell. I had no reason to trust either my eyes or my judgment.

Sometimes, believe it or not, a detective's best friend is a pencil and paper. You have to know what questions to ask if you want to get anywhere.

After about twenty minutes of dickering with myself, pacing around the room, and scrawling a bunch of half-formed ideas on the paper, I got something I could work with.

1. *What made Sam go for a drive after he got back into the house?*
2. *Why did his car go over the cliff?*
3. *Did anyone else see the ghost?*
4. *For that matter, what's the deal with the whole haunting business?*
5. *Assuming this wasn't a suicide or an accident, who would want to kill him? And why?*
6. *What's the deal with Sam's phone call last night?*
7. *What else am I not asking?*

That last one is a question that makes it on to every list, written or not. It's the most important question—it's always the question you don't ask that lands you in a dirty public bathroom with a gun to your head when you thought you were picking up a date.

Not that I'd know what that's like.

4:30 PM, MONDAY

IN THE WINTER IN THE NORTHWEST, night doesn't ever really fall. It horns in from the Arctic Circle and shoves the day south, then settles over the benighted land like a celestial goat straining with constipation. After about four thirty in the afternoon, there was nothing up there but a blank red-black where the city lights bounced off the overcast.

The mercury on the ancient front-porch weather station still didn't reach thirty-two—the world would remain frozen tonight, but if it didn't snow again, the runways at SEA-TAC might be open tomorrow.

Assuming I could get the charge thrown out at my hearing, I could be home in twenty-four hours. Maybe less. Back in the land where the hills marked the seasons with a gentle swing between emerald and gold, with a lot of dingy in between.

I could see Samantha pacing back and forth on the driveway, never quite daring to approach the spot where Sam died.

One deep breath—and a cough to clear the cold air's itching out of the bottom of my lungs. Then, plunge in.

She didn't react to my approach. I paced her.

"Samantha?"

"Don't talk to me."

"Okay."

I walked next to her, quiet. I counted the steps. Noted the patterns that her breath drew in the corner of my vision.

Five minutes later:

"What do you want, Clarke?"

"Forget it. You don't want to talk. You probably want to kill me."

"You have no idea."

Another minute or two.

"Look, please, either go away or talk."

"You never could bear silence."

"Oh, I learned." A voice as cold as the air. "God, I learned."

"I'm sorry."

"You should be."

"Maybe. I need to ask you something."

"Haven't you done enough already?" She blamed me for the way her life turned out. Or for Sam's death. Or both.

"No."

"God, just go away, will you?"

"Sam," it was a dirty trick using her nickname—remind her of a more familiar time and of her husband's death together, but it was all I had. "I need to know what you saw."

"What?"

"The car. What did you see?"

"Get lost." She burrowed further back into her coat, and fixed her eyes on the ground a few feet in front of her. I wasn't going to get anything out of her this way.

INSIDE, THE MANSION *FELT* haunted. I didn't have a better word for it. That sense of death had come to the House of Lantham, thick as a heavy fog in the hallways. Even though I knew better—or thought I did—I expected a lion to leap out at me from every shadow.

I found Tom first, taking a joyless meal in the otherwise empty dining room. I tapped on the door frame, he just about jumped out of his skin. I didn't blame him, I was ready to jump out of mine.

"Tom, got a minute?"

He clutched at his chest like I'd just zapped him into full-on angina. "I suppose."

"Thanks. Look, I know it's the last thing you want to think about, but I've got to know what happened when Sam came back into the house."

"Oh." He sighed, took his glasses off and spent a very careful time folding them, like he was trying to intimidate me by showing them who was boss. Same move he pulled when he told me I wasn't good enough for his daughter. Some things don't change. "When I got into the house he had already disappeared. I felt it was best to err on the side of caution, so I went to find the children in the TV room playing video games. They invited me to play—golf, they were playing. So I showed Jimmy how to keep from slicing his swing. The next thing I knew, maybe five minutes later, maybe less, the maid showed up looking like death..."

"So you didn't speak to him, or know why he went for a drive?"

"No. I have no idea." He leaned forward on his elbows and pressed his lips against his tented forefingers. "Why are you asking this?"

"Should I be asking something different?"

"Perhaps. Perhaps you should be asking why he would kill himself."

"You think it was a suicide?"

"I'm certain it was."

"Why?"

"Oh, now, surely you noticed that this house is not the bastion of love and tranquility that Samuel pretended it was?"

"I did."

"You thought it a coincidence?"

"No," I stepped to the table and took a seat, as it seemed I was in for a long one. "It was pretty much what I expected from what I remembered of Sam."

"Then you are even less intelligent than I thought you were.."

"Enlighten me."

"Edith and I aren't here for the holidays. We came here last month to support our daughter."

"Why?"

"Can't you guess? It may have taken me a long time to understand your brother, but I'll wager I understand him better than you ever did."

"Couldn't fake it anymore?"

"As you say. He was not satisfied performing to his talents. He needed to prove himself, continually. In the early years, he was a good husband and father. He performed his professional duties adequately—as his superior, I had no complaints, but there was very little astonishing about him. He could have had a comfortable career with a good retirement, as a customer service liaison or manager.

"Unfortunately, there are men in this world who confuse mediocrity with unfulfilled potential."

"How do you mean?"

"He was not satisfied, and he took that to mean he was meant for something greater. He campaigned for years for a promotion to our investment division—I'll admit to you, in my shame, that he wore me down, and I promoted him farther than I should. I fear that, in the end, his death was my responsibility." I didn't see any tears. His face had that kind of hard cast that men develop when they're used to hiding unpleasant feelings. But he wasn't flinching.

"How is it your responsibility?"

"There were quotas, and standards, in his position. I would only protect him for so long if he didn't perform, and he knew that. I underestimated the lengths he would go to to avoid losing face."

I raised an eyebrow. He nodded.

"What did he do?"

"He improved. All of a sudden, his revenues went through the roof. Impressive deals. He displayed the most canny sense of market timing, an uncharacteristically astute understanding of his whole field. I checked up, he'd been taking advantage of the advanced training we offered. I thought he'd finally found his place."

"So what happened?" I wished he'd just get to the point, but I knew he wouldn't. He needed the power over timing on a day when he was powerless in every possible way. I didn't have a good reason to do more than gently prod at this point.

"Our legal department received subpoenas from a grand jury. The SEC, FTC, the whole alphabet soup took a keen interest in his activities." Tighter voice, a little red creeping in, but not much. He'd be a good poker player—but he was clearly livid. "Insider trading, derivatives trading against company policy, and fraud. When I confronted him this morning, he didn't take it well."

"Didn't take it well?"

"He tried to blackmail me."

"With...?"

"He said he would tell the government that he was acting at my direction."

"And was he?"

"Excuse me?" Tom looked like he'd just discovered that his dinner was made of dog turds.

"Was he following orders?"

"Absolutely not!" Tom slammed his fist on the table.

"I'm sorry, Tom. I had to be sure."

"Why?"

"I'm..." I stopped. What he didn't know couldn't hurt me. "I mean, he was my brother. There's an obligation, right?"

Tom lifted a glass of white to his lips and harrumphed at it, then sipped. As far as he was concerned, that was the end of it.

At the door to the kitchen, I paused. "Oh, Tom, what can you tell me about the haunting?"

He choked on his food. Spluttered. Caught his breath. Then, like a hyena, just about doubled over with his face in his food.

"I say something funny?"

He kept laughing, shook his head, and waved me away.

One vote against the haunting, then.

And at least some possible answers for the questions on my list.

Malfeasance and fraud are hefty accusations—should be easy to verify, if I had a few days and the budget to hire Earl Whitaker, which I didn't. I'd need some more direct intelligence, and that would have to wait until everyone else was asleep.

In the kitchen, Cynthia looked about as perky as a plate of badly reheated asparagus. When she saw me, all the greeting I got was a look that said something along the lines of "If I have to deal with any more shit from these people today, someone else is gonna wind up dead."

I plunged in to the rinse-and-dry pile, and started scrubbing. "This brings back memories."

"Good?"

"Repressed."

"Ah. Those are the best kind." She passed me another pot for my rinse pile. "It's not a bad job, most of the time."

"You're the only one here?"

"Family in Kansas, we don't celebrate Christmas together."

"Hmph. Sounds like my kind of family."

"You converted to Judaism?"

"Okay, not my kind of family." I buffed the water spots out of a wine glass. "Why not put these through the washer?"

"Waterford. Sammy has...had...a firm hand-wash-only policy."

"Hmph. Good old Sam." I set the glass down. "Thanks for the help earlier."

"*De nada.*"

"Good, strong grasp of Hebrew."

"Oh, shut up." She splashed me, giggling openly.

"Okay, okay." I'd nearly found the bottom of my rinse pile. "I gotta ask you something kind of morbid."

"What could possibly make this day more morbid?"

"I need to know what you saw when...well, when Sam died."

"Oh." She focused tight on her hands, used the washing ritual as an anchor. Her voice quavered. "Mostly I remember the blood all over the snow. Trying to hold him back, keep him from killing you, or Mrs. Lantham."

"What about after?"

"He...he came out of the garage like a maniac, and crashed."

"Did you see the crash?"

"I...he just kind of floated sideways. Like in slow motion. Is it always like that?"

"Usually." I kept my eyes on her, but didn't pause in the

drying. Her words came on the beat of the scrubs. You don't interrupt that kind of rhythm, not in someone who's not used to violence. "Everything slows down. Can you remember exactly what you saw?"

She took a breath, closed her eyes. She didn't stop washing—her fingers judged the grime by touch. "He must be driving at forty, fifty miles an hour."

"That's good. Watch it happen. Tell me what you see."

"He's turning the corner onto the main driveway, and...and...no, that can't be right."

"What?"

"I can swear...somebody pushed him."

"Who?"

"I...you...I don't believe it."

"Don't worry. Just tell me."

"A man in a hat just...appeared. The car started to slide. And then he disappeared. That's not possible."

"Anything else?"

"I can swear...god, it's crazy, but I can swear I heard thunder." She was shaking. Tears. Time for her adrenaline dump. Textbook. "God, I'm such a wuss." She wiped her eyes with her forearms, like a raccoon trying to wash its face.

I wiped my left hand dry and gently gripped the back of her neck. "It's okay. It's normal."

"Really?"

"You saw me in the shower. What do you think?"

She snuffled, and smiled. Relief. No doubt.

"You think it was the ghost?"

"I don't believe in ghosts."

"That's not what I asked."

She crossed her arms over her chest. Examined the dishwater again. "No, I don't think it was. But that's what I saw. God help me. I swear, that's what I saw."

6:30 PM, MONDAY

ANOTHER HOUR MUDDLING AROUND didn't get me much of anything. As delightful as I found the wild ghost chase and the pursuit of family tranquility, I had other issues. Like court in the morning. At nine o'clock. In Seattle. And my ride was dead, which kind of put a crimp in my plans.

I stopped back by my room to take care of a few odds and ends. Email from Rachael, update on Southland. Why was she working today?

Cab pickup, bloody expensive. Rental car, on the company's dime this time. Then, an email to make sure my character witness would file his friend-of-the-court brief on time.

A bit of poking around on the net for good old Officer Bellman. Not a guy shy about getting in the headlines. Seemed like the kind of cop who'd beaten his head bloody against the bureaucracy until he gave up. Reading between the lines, looked like he'd had a half-dozen high profile collars snatched out from under him. He had a love of detective novels, judging by his Amazon account. Forty-five, still working the street when other cops had been promoted up and out to investigations.

Officer Bellman might just prove useful.

Now, burn the shots of the accident from my phone to a CD. Grab a few odds and ends for the pockets in case I got a chance to do more snooping in my insomnia hours. And the phone...

"Lantham Investigations. We snoop and scoop your poop." She giggled. At least I caught her in a good mood.

"Rachael, you still at work?"

"Oh, no, nothing, just..." music blared in the background. "Just a movie night."

"Hmph. A movie night, huh? At the office?"

"You should be here. We're doing toenails." Ah, the sound that every cop at a sobriety checkpoint dreams of—a blood alcohol content of .12 or better. "Your pet primate has the wildest colors and...no, no, not the feet!"

"Oh, god."

The giggles subsided. "You said it, buster! What does you want anyhow?"

"Just checking in. Everything okay down there?"

"Ev'rthin's purrrrfect. Donald! More! Oh, Lantham you should see what I see. I gotta go. Happy Jews-Go-To-The-Movies Day!"

Click.

The responsible manager and businessman in me made a note to have a talk with her about appropriate use of company offices and resources. The rest of me would far rather have been in a den of drink and laughter and sudden comedic nudity than stuck in this misplaced icebox. Granted, with a crowd younger than I preferred, but the desperate don't comparison shop.

Six thirty PM. Two hours after dark, and the night hadn't even started. Tomorrow's datebook called for me to wake up bright and surly, but I was about as likely to actually fall asleep as my brother was to rise from the dead, and this was the wrong holiday for that.

Insomnia. What a bitch. Sure, I had a case and even a twenty-five cent retainer, but warm and fuzzy and full of purpose? I wasn't feeling it. This particular ostentatious flea-bag wasn't the kind of flophouse that made me want to spend eight hours dancing with the Sandman.

I packed up my laptop. If I was gonna be working late I might as well do it somewhere with a view of a Christmas tree.

CHRISTMAS: TIME OF ALCOHOLISM, deforestation, creepy relatives, teen pregnancy, ghost stories, unlikely astrology, and the last-ditch effort to prop up the books for the end of the fiscal year. So far, I was down one creepy relative and up one ghost story, which gave me two points—well on the way to being one of the better Christmases I'd had in the last few years when all I could boast from the list was situational alcoholism.

I half-expected to find company sitting in the creepy room in front of the Christmas tree. For a house with children, this Lantham enclave continued in its eerie perpetual silence. Maybe tonight it made sense.

I'd already managed—unintentionally—to kill my brother. You'd think that slaughtering few hours would be a no-brainer.

No-brainer, that's Detective Lantham in a nutshell.

A gorgeous antique scrimshaw chess set on the end table. I played a few games against myself to limber up the synapses, but I kept losing. The lights on the Christmas tree, which I normally would have found soothing, didn't do anything but annoy me as they chased each other like inane rabbits through a fox gauntlet. I could use something to help me unwind.

Like music. A little music would be just the thing.

I took the remote from the slot on the side of the coffee table and pointed it at the armoire next to the door and powered the system on, then pressed play on the off-chance that there might be something palatable in the CD player.

Nothing. That figured. I got up and paced back and forth a few times. Stretch out the muscles. Hop up and down a bit, remind the heart that it's supposed to be keeping up its end of the cardiovascular bargain. Try to get the hairs on the back of my neck to quit standing up. The fire was going strong in the fireplace, but I swear to you I could feel cold fingers reaching in through that broken window and running down my spine from cranium to butt-crack.

Music. Yeah. I could swear I heard the CD player spinning, too. Probably just nerves, right?

A once-top-of-the-line-and-still-would-put-George-Lucas's-poodle's-to-shame hi-fi receiver lived in the armoire at the top of a component rack, above which an impressive collection of CDs and vinyl arranged themselves in perfect alphabetical order. I thumbed through, decided on a bit of Chumbawamba for the sheer dorky nostalgia value, and opened the CD carousel.

The display on the CD player showed a disc active. And playing. On repeat. Weird. I checked the volume—was set at maximum, the CD channel was active, but no music. No sound at all.

Rotate the carousel until Chumbawamba was active. A gold, unlabeled disc swung out.

"Hello, what's this?" I put my right pinky into the spindle hole and picked it up. The business side of the disc had been burned all the way out to the edges. Two seconds later, the sound of Chumbawamba at volume eleven knocked me down, but I got up again and managed to squelch it before I lost what was left of my suddenly-diminished hearing.

Turning back from the armoire, my heart went zero-for-two. Samantha stood in the doorway looking like the short love child of a vulture and a gargoyle.

"Do you mind keeping it down?"

I mumbled an apology, served it with a chaser about the stereo being set too high.

"Fine. The kids just went to bed. Can you keep it down?"

"Yeah, no problem." I turned back to the stereo to turn it down a little more, then killed the extra banks of speakers, just for safety.

"Good." She blew by me and poked at the fire as if it had personally killed her husband.

I set back down and deployed my computer, keeping the CD poised on the end of my finger: no extraneous prints. Paranoid? Maybe. But I hate things that don't fit, and the CD didn't fit. Neither did a ghost pushing a car into a gully, but this seemed like a more manageable puzzle.

The computer insisted it was a data CD, not audio. One file, big enough to take up the whole CD. A .wav—uncompressed audio. A lecture? Why not just burn it as an audio CD if you were going to put it in the stereo?

I tried playing it, but all I got was silence. Not even white noise, just blank silence.

Samantha slammed the poker against a log and swore.

"Need something?"

"I...no. Dammit..." She dropped the poker on the granite tilework. Wringing her hands like dirty laundry.

I ignored her and opened up a sound editor on the grounds that nobody burns 70 minutes of complete silence. Maybe the file was damaged at the beginning—component players aren't exactly renowned for their robust firmware.

Yeah, that was a valid sound file all right. The waveform was filled almost to clip with what looked like two oscillating signals overlaid on each other. Left and right channel seemed to be offset enough that, assuming they were pure tones, they would cancel each other out to zero periodically, maybe every minute or two.

I zoomed in to time index zero. No damage. I checked the file headers. They looked fine—even ffplay didn't spit back a single error. Whatever monkeyshines gave birth to this soundless sonic experiment, the result was exactly as intended.

And...why?

Samantha was trying to get my attention again. Note to any of you who might find yourself needing to talk to a brother-in-law who you resent more than you can articulate: if you want to get listened to, try English (or whatever other actually-spoken language is appropriate to your hometown). "Huffgrumblefretandstomp" is not a language that anyone puts out correspondence courses for. I was in the middle of what, so far, looked to be a fairly masturbatory form of forensics, and wasn't really impressed by the number of different ways she could sigh.

I split the tracks and looked at the waveform. Definitely synthesized, both channels—completely regular from one peak to another, even scrubbing to the end of the file. None of the sharp attacks or peaks that you'd expect from speech or Foley or a natural instrument.

Samantha gave up and tried English. "Clarke?"

"What?" I didn't look at her.

"I...well...Clarke, what am I going to do?"

"Plan a funeral, file the insurance claim. The normal things people do..."

"No, I mean...what am I going to *do*?"

I closed the laptop. "You go on. You live."

"Ha. You make it sound easy."

"It's not. But it is simple." I shrugged and opened the computer again.

"Look, I know I don't have any right. God knows I don't have any right to ask you for anything..."

She started pacing. I'd been expecting this one, but I didn't really know how I'd react. On a wall in the back of my mind, I always kept a very small torch lit—though I wouldn't have admitted it to myself without large quantities of extra-rancid bourbon.

"Clarke, have you ever thought about us?"

"Of course."

"The kids love you, and..."

"No."

"What?"

I ripped my attention away from the laptop again and looked her in the eye. "I said 'no.'"

"No...no?"

"No, I don't want to pick things up where we left off. I don't want to go to bed with you tonight. I don't want to stay here and help you through this difficult time. No matter how you phrase it, the answer's no."

"But...don't you..."

"Yes. Or I did. But that doesn't really matter, does it?" Her jaw hung open, like I was speaking Punjabi. "Eleven years ago I wouldn't leave my job for you, I'm not going to do it now."

"You wouldn't have to, there's plenty of crime up here."

"Up here? No offense, sweetheart, but I have a home somewhere you can see the sun more than thirty-five days a year. I have friends, and a business that you don't just pack up and move. I have a life I enjoy..." I stumbled as I realized I actually meant it—amazing how much that can shake you when you're used to a certain high baseline of misery, "so, like I said, the answer is no. I'm sorry."

"Clarke," she stood next to me and ran her hand along the side of my head. My scrotum puckered. It had been a while, and she was my first. Late start. Good memories. "I've missed you."

For maybe twenty seconds, I let her touch me. When you're lucky enough to do the job you love, you get used to living alone, get used to the things it gives you. You can go for months, maybe years without someone touching you like this. You can forget that anyone ever did, or what it did to you. You forget that sex is another kind of hunger, and your hand is the nutritional equivalent of Taco Bell. You get scared, because the last time you had it, nobody agreed what it meant.

But the last time I'd had Samantha, she broke my heart. Not because she left me, either. You get dumped, it hurts, that's life. I knew that at twenty-three when I met her. I knew it at twenty-four when I left her.

No. She broke my heart because she used to want to make something out of herself. Knew that she wanted to run a charter service for marine tours. Batty? Maybe, but she wanted it every inch as much as I wanted to be a cop. And she gave it up because her parents didn't approve.

When that happened, it was just a matter of time before I left. You can't stay with someone you don't respect—and you can't love someone you can't respect. She made her choices, I made mine. That's life.

"Samantha," I took her hand, removed it from my head, and pushed it against her leg. I stood up. "It was over eleven years ago. It's just as over now. No take-backs. No do-overs. Go to bed, try to get some sleep. You're going to have a lot of shit to deal with tomorrow. Those kids'll need you."

"You're cold."

"It goes with the job."

She backed away from me, realized she was backing into the tree, then skirted the table, facing me as she retreated from the room.

I kept half an eye on her, in case she got the inclination to throw something. She disappeared up the front hall, heading god-knew-where.

Fine with me.

Now, waveform: Deliberate, check. Left on repeat in the stereo, check. Doesn't play a damn thing, check. Was it rodent repellent? High frequencies can work for that. Cats are better, but Sam was allergic.

Human hearing ranges more or less from 20hz to 20khz—sounds to scare off rodents and dogs hover up around 22 to 26khz. I pulled up the spectral analysis, but all the signal was pushed hard to the left, bunching up around 12hz, tailing down to 6hz, and hitting a hard shelf at 15hz. The kind of frequencies they push in movie theaters to make explosions thump you in the chest. You can feel it, but you can't hear it, and it's so low that it takes a hard pulse for it to really register. These kind of soft oscillations in this waveform were just useless. No good for vermin, no use on humans, too constant to be good for atmosphere.

Weird.

Maybe Sam had been trying some kind of binaural meditation crap to help with the stress of being a people-pleasing soulless felon with a cover-up he couldn't handle. Wouldn't be the first time he went in for fashionable mysticism.

A cover-up? Well, no time like the present to go on another snoop. This time I had my bag of tricks with me.

I pulled a thumb drive and my "borrowed" set of keys from the laptop case and stole around the corner and down a few doors to Sam's office. Insert, twist, push, enter, close. A half-empty bottle of Maker's Mark and an abandoned tumbler on the desk, still alcohol in it by the smell, but not much. About right for something standing since just before Sam came out to pick a fight. Depending on how many he'd had, this might just be an accident after all.

Yeah, I bought that like I bought Midol to relieve my PMS.

The terminal was still locked. No problem tonight.

I reached under the desk and toggled the power supply cut-off on the back of the tower. Pulled the mouse out, stuck my drive into the freshly-empty USB port. Now, power-up. Quick side-trip into the BIOS to check the boot order. Boot to the memory stick.

The little flash drive had a custom Slackware build with a few little extras, courtesy Earl Whitaker. It brought me up to an unassuming command prompt, all drives mounted.

I typed "pilfer email /dev/hda ; pilfer /dev/hda *.doc *.xls *.pdf ; pilfer sql odbc access" and hit enter. It wouldn't grab everything, but it would give me enough to maybe get an idea for the scope of Sam's problem. If he was involved in a failing cover-up, there was a chance that his co-conspirators were sensible enough to knock him off before he could make a deal with the Feds to roll over. If nothing else, this should give me their names.

Estimated time to completion: two hours. The boy still couldn't throw anything away. Bad for his posthumous reputation, good for my peace of mind. Going home unsure of why he died wasn't a notion that got my genitals all warm and flushed.

MIDNIGHT SNACK? DON'T MIND if I do. The lack of dinner in my personal galaxy had me running like an eighty-year-old mule with malnutrition. A few hundred calories, and maybe something to wet my whistle, might get my neurons firing again.

In the fridge I found an unused Christmas dinner, so carved myself a bit of ham and warmed it with some potatoes and a slice of cherry pie. The kitchen was too big to feel homey, so I retreated to the living room and set up with my laptop. A few minutes with something appropriately festive before I got down to work could have been nice, but I resisted the temptation to pull up the official *Twilight Zone* archive. I had enough of that kind of thing in real life.

So, subsonics. I wouldn't have kept bothering with it except that every time I'd gotten the feeling of slugs crawling up the small of my back this weekend, it had been strongest in this room—it wasn't just because of the cold air through hole in the window or the Christmas tree, and it wasn't because Samantha had been playing *Andy Williams's Christmas Album* non-stop—she hadn't. Come to think of it, I hadn't heard any Christmas music, or any music at all, in the house all weekend.

The Oracle of Geek-Fu—Google—insisted that the only interesting thing called "Subsonics" on the Internet was a garage band out of Atlanta. Nothing in the film or music rags I subscribed to either. "Binaural meditation"—a flavor of popular nonsense that a particular client claimed had helped her cope with the guilt associated with knifing her best friend's poodle last year—turned up a few hundred entrepreneurial dealers of fashionable woo desperate to convince me that my brain needed a kind of entertainment that real life simply couldn't provide.

It might have been right about that. I hadn't gotten laid in at least eight months.

But nothing about a subsonic twist on that particular fad. Damn.

"Uncle Clark?" Sarah's small voice just about made me jump out of my skin like it was a cheap set of coveralls. "Is it true?"

She stood in the doorway, not meeting my eyes, swaying this way and that. A stuffed rabbit dangled by one ear from her left hand. Her right pulled the whole left arm tight against her side, like she was afraid it would fall off.

"Is what true?"

"Did you kill my Daddy?"

"No. Come here." I patted the couch next to me. One of those antique Victorian-style couches, still in the original upholstery. Never enough pillows.

She curled up at the end of the couch, hugged her knees, looked over them at me. A tenuous trust. Easy to shatter.

"Your Daddy and I got in a fight. He was mad. He'd been drinking. You've heard adults talk about how you can't drive if you've been drinking?"

"Yeah."

"He decided to go for a drive. He drove too fast, and his car crashed. Your mom is mad at me for fighting with him."

Her brow crinkled, like she couldn't decide whether to hate me or forgive me. "Why did you fight?"

"Don't you sometimes fight with your brothers?"

"Yeah."

"Your Mom gets you to try to make up?"

"Yeah."

"You should listen to her. Your Daddy and I used to fight all the time. We've been mad at each other for a long time. We didn't listen to our Mom when she told us to forgive each other."

"Why not?"

"Sometimes, people make mistakes."

"Oh."

She peered at me from behind her knees. Something else on her mind?

"Sarah, is that why you came down?"

"No."

"What's the matter?"

"It's back. *He's* back." She whispered it. Afraid the walls would hear. "The ghost."

There it was again. The ghost everyone seemed to know

about, but only Sarah would talk about in any detail. "Did you hear him?"

She shook her head. "I *saw* him. Down on the driveway."

"What was he doing?"

She shrugged and laid her head on her knees.

"Sarah, what are you doing out of bed?" Cynthia, probably following the smell of dinner. She swept in and picked the little girl up under both arms. Two slippered feet thumped the ground. "Off you go. No getting back out of bed."

"Yes ma'am." Sarah scurried out and around the corner.

"Thanks." I returned my attention to my dinner.

"Don't like kids?"

I speared a hunk of ham. "I like 'em fine." I chomped, "Long as I've got a good Dijon to go with them."

"Meow." She sat down next to me. Lovely. I had apparently been elected to the position of house estrogen relief therapist. If Edith came down, I'd have to start charging an hourly rate.

"Eh. Been a long day. What do you need?"

"Me? I was saving that child from an untimely end as a barbecue."

"Her father wound up as a milkshake this afternoon."

"More than enough fast food for one day, don't you think?"

I chuckled and had a nibble of the green beans almondine. "Fair 'nuff. You make this?"

"Mm. You're looking at the whole kitchen staff this week."

"Well, technically," I took another bite and pointed my fork at the screen, "I'm looking at sound engineering tech articles."

"Speaking of which," she bent over and untied her shoes, then pulled her knees up under her, "you owe me dinner."

I held up another forkful of food. "Rain check?"

"I suppose."

"Let me ask you something, this ghost..."

She grunted, like trying to keep back a laugh.

"I say something funny?"

"Not at all." More smiles than talking silverware in a Disney film. She shifted, throwing a leg behind me.

"What are you...ooh, that's nice. Smithers, massage my brain."

She answered by kneading my skull like the dough-ball the day had turned it into. *Relax, Lantham, relax.*

"Is everyone in bed?" I groaned happily.

"I think so. Last person I saw go up was Edith."

"Where are you staying, anyway?"

"Servant's quarters, near the office. I sleep in there when they need me to stay over and help with the kids."

"Mm. Did you hear anyone go out?"

"No. Why?"

"Sarah's seeing ghosts."

"Don't worry about it. She's been seeing them for days. I think it's my fault."

"Oh? That's nice. Keep that up." She started working at my shoulders. Another few minutes of this and I'd have to rethink that side business in selling surplus knots to hobby sailors. "Why is the ghost your fault?"

"I read them..."

"Them?"

"The children. I read them *A Christmas Carol.*"

"I think my brain has turned to mush. Connect the dots?"

"They were having a camp-out in the TV room. After I left Jimmy started telling stories about the gangster murders that happened here. Between him and Albert, Sarah wound up having nightmares all night. Ever since, she's been swearing she's seeing ghosts." She squeezed down my arms.

"She claims the ghost is keeping her awake—came to see

me last night, and again tonight. I thought it was just a sleepy kid..."

"Except we saw it today."

"Yeah." It's hard to think straight when you're being assaulted with relaxation. "It's like a bad dream, and one that left the factory before it got QC'd. God, I hate things that don't add up."

"That's why you're a detective?"

"Among other reasons. That's nice. Keep that up." She stroked my arms from wrists back up to scalp. I thought about pushing her off, but my brain was tied in as many knots as my back. Free relaxation and dinner—sometimes that's what it takes to get the old synapses firing again. *Fall back into it, Lantham. Free break time. No lions in the dark.* "Hmm...lions."

"Huh?"

"Oh, was just thinking that for the first time this weekend I don't feel like a lion's going to jump me from behind."

"Someone must've turned off the heater."

"Heater?"

"Mm...the thing rumbles like a lion." Her fingers trailed over my ears and along my jawline. "Always gives me the heebie jeebies. You okay?"

"Yeah. Just been a while."

When it's been a while, you start to wonder if performance anxiety is the thing that's gonna trip you up. Don't worry about it. Sex is like riding a bike—as long as you don't pitch forward over the handlebars and break your nose, you'll probably muddle through.

You do tend to forget things. Smells. Tastes. Textures. I'd forgotten the itch I get in the arch of my left foot when someone drags their fingernails along the underside of my arms. They're the kinds of things you want to forget—some things come best as a surprise.

Trouble is, if your name is Clarke Lantham, you also tend to forget about things like gravity and inertia, or that at the end of a week in the ninth circle of hell your balance is about as useful as a pogo stick on an ice rink.

In such situations, removing a pair of pants can turn into a major engineering challenge, and it doesn't help matters when you get the order mixed up. You're liable to wind up accidentally sitting on the coffee table in your dinner, with a pair of panties tangled up around your head and trying to find the proper spots to nibble by touch alone. And when she tries to help you out, you can sometimes wind up pitching backward over the table and sprawling across the floor.

My nose got a bit wet for the best possible undignified reason, and it wanted to kill me for exacerbating its fight wounds, but I didn't break it. Just like riding a bike.

She didn't seem to mind. And, in an unusual stroke of forethought, I'd managed to shift so that the laptop was out of immediate danger.

Aside from the tumbling, we managed not to make enough noise to worry abou. At least we didn't wake the house.

It took a few minutes of pleasant roasting in front of the fire before the giggle fits let up.

I traced spirals on her hip while I caught my breath. "Bonobo handshake? Hell of a way to say hi."

"Pleased to meet you, Detective Lantham."

HALF AN HOUR LATER, I RETRIEVED the USB stick and returned the office to the state in which I'd found it, then gave Cynthia the key ring and a last kiss before getting back to work.

A cursory look told me I was going to be at this all night. The boy never got into the habit of clearing spam out of his inbox.

On the other hand, his bad technological hygiene meant that he hadn't discovered the usefulness of cryptography. His life, such as it was, was an open book.

What I needed was an index. I set my machine to build one of every word used in the whole archive of files. Another hour of sitting around on my ass, trying to figure out the rest.

My phone beeped. Text message. Rachael.

Southland stakeout wrapped up. Inside job. Client unhappy, promises to raise hell over expenses. Nya proved useful. Details when you get home.

What the hell, a consult doesn't hurt.

To Rachael:

Coming up dry on some subsonics research. Any idea who uses them outside of the movies?

The reply came quick as a fifteen-year-old boy.

Fuck subsonics. Try infrasound. Big in earthquake prediction.

Infrasound? There was a new one.

Wikipedia, here I come.

Blah blah earthquake prediction research blah blah seismology blah blah human reactions to infrasound. Bingo.

"Infrasound has been known to cause feelings of awe or fear in humans. Since it is not consciously perceived, it can make people feel vaguely that supernatural events are taking place."

Induced haunting? It linked to a paper called *The Ghost in the Machine*, which documented the presence of infrasound in several haunted sites and linked it to vague hallucinations, irritability, unease, the whole bit.

If I'd had to describe the way the house made me feel since the moment I got here, I'd have come up with that paper.

But it wasn't just this room. Oh, it was strongest in this room, at least sometimes, but the whole house felt this way—and not just when the heater was on. If I was going to fake a haunting, I'd want to hook this thing up to something structural. A heating duct, maybe, or the sewer pipes.

I scootched the armoire out a few inches, traced the speaker cables.

Two sets. One to the surround sound rig in this room. One stereo pair running down through the floor. Did this place have a basement?

Only one way to find out.

The house was a custom, not a floor plan I was familiar with. Best to start with the stairwells.

The one at this end of the house was a no-go. No doors that I could find leading down. The south corridor, though, had what I had assumed was a broom closet. It opened on to an unfinished wooden staircase leading down.

A light switch at the top gave me a couple hanging bare

bulbs showing the way down to what, at the base of the stairs at least, proved to be a wine cellar. The bottles were not the most interesting part of the view.

At least a month's worth of dust coated the stairs completely, except for the boot prints. Two sets only—one ascending, one descending. A handrail on either side meant I could perch and shimmy down on my hands without disturbing the footprints in the dust.

The dust on the two racks standing opposite the foot of the stairs told the same story—a month of dust, maybe two. Most of the wine hadn't been touched in longer—a lot longer. A squint at a couple of the labels explained why: expensive stuff, long-term storage. Probably only ever touched at New Year's, if that.

Except for the ass-end of the wine cellar, the rest of the basement looked well-kept. A deep freeze and shelves of canned and dried goods clustered around another staircase toward the back of the house—probably led up to the kitchen. No trace of the deep dust I'd seen on the other stairs.

The basement, though, wasn't as big as the house. A cinder block wall with evenly spaced ceiling and floor vents closed off the room, limiting it to the back half of the house. Wide, boxy air ducts spidered out from the wall to all corners of the house.

The door in the middle of the wall didn't have a lock on it. Behind, the furnace, with plenty of breathing space.

A check of the northwest corner showed a pair of speaker wires running into the room from the ceiling, then along the backside of a floor strut until it reached the furnace.

Two long-throw subwoofers, about ten inchers, tacked to the back side of the main heating duct, offset by insulating studs to keep them from melting. Pipe that CD's sound down here? Instant haunted house.

A shine of my cell phone's screen showed me a dust

coating along the speaker's top ridges, just about as thick as the stuff that survived in the footprints on the stairs.

So, whoever mounted the speakers had come in through the less-used south entrance. And had left a signature. Probably a member of the household, or a frequent visitor, which cut my number of suspects from the previous pool by precisely zero.

I took some shots of the speakers, and of the tracks on the stairs, before heading back up to base camp through the kitchen entrance.

So, Lantham, cards on the table. What the hell is going on in this crazy house?

Someone was faking a haunting—as a cover for murder? That seemed obvious.

But why?

Five suspects. Five motives. I discounted myself because I knew I didn't do it.

Samantha looked the best for this grisly little affair. A man with the kind of obscene income that would afford this house would've been insured within an inch of the sky. If a certain darling husband took a tumble, a certain darling wife would recoup enough cash to pay off an underwater house, maybe run her own life away from parental micromanagement. A bit late to finally grow a spine, but better late than never.

Tom looked pretty good too. Sam's shenanigans had brought the DOJ down on his bank, putting him in a situation where revenge would be extra convenient. The miscreant takes the fall, the investigation dead-ends. Saves the public humiliation of Sam being brought to trial—and that was assuming that Tom wasn't in on the malfeasance in the first place. A lot of people in his business made a lot of money before the derivatives market collapsed, and most of that was insider trading. You have to follow these things when you're chasing insurance jobs—a lot of the jobs going begging were in the mortgage sector.

Cynthia didn't look quite as good, but she certainly bore Sam no great affection. Between the sexual harassment and her general contempt for him as a human being, she wasn't exactly broken up about seeing him smashed to soup.

Edith, maybe another rung down the ladder. If she'd done it, her motives would be personal. Classic vigilant mother, looks out too much for her baby. If she knew how miserable Samantha was, she might have seen it as a way to help out. But I didn't buy it. Everything I knew about Edith told me that it just wasn't in her to be this cold—she'd more likely help Samantha dig up dirt on Sam so the custody hearings would go the right way. Far as I could see, Edith didn't have another motive. She wasn't a part of the banking world, she had her own thing going as a champion rose breeder.

And Sam. Always a chance it could have been a suicide. This one was still a big question mark, at least until I finished chewing through the rest of his files. As a rank act of cowardice it fit, but what a messy way to go—and why fake a haunting to cover it up? And how did he arrange for the ghost to appear in front of everyone out in the yard, where the infrasound wouldn't have been affecting us anyway? And how did at least two of us see the same thing: the image of a man in a hat and overcoat, like a prohibition-era gangster? The papers on infrasound described the hallucinations that people had as "gray blobs in the corner of the eye." Maybe like what Samantha had seen when she busted the window, but not like what we'd seen out front.

The computer needed another twenty minutes to chew through everything. Where could I find a flashlight in a house like this? Coat closet in the entryway?

Worth a try.

Two Mag-Lites and a hand light on the top shelf. Fresh batteries even—privileges of having a staff of servants. I took the heftiest one on the off chance that I ran into an unexpectedly corporeal "ghost" out in the cold and dim.

The driveway was navigable enough by the solar-powered footlights that lined it every six feet or so. No fog tonight, though the overcast still hung low enough to paint everything a dull gray-red. I kept my Mag-Lite off 'til I got to the grotesque quadruple gash the car had carved through the lawn and hedge.

Black scars through the white. Obscene death metal graffiti. I started at the edge of the pavement, but I didn't follow the tracks into the gully. Been there, done that, got the blood sausage. What interested me was what was in the other direction. I put my back to the crash site and got my bearings. Facing dead in line with the trajectory of the crash, the doorstep was just shy of my twelve o'clock. Maybe eleven forty-five. That's where I'd been. From where I'd been, it'd looked like he'd suddenly gone sideways off the road.

Pushed by a ghost? Yeah, and my toes used to dance the Nutcracker with the San Francisco Ballet.

Where had the rest of them been standing? I swept left about twenty degrees and turned the light on. The snow would be a disaster from the god-awful scuffle this afternoon. Just thinking about that made my face hurt again. There, at about ten o'clock.

So the ghost illusion—it had to be an illusion—would need to sell from both vantage points.

Question was, how?

From my vantage, the ghost appeared right next to the car, for a quarter second or less. A shadow, dull but distinct in the diffuse daylight.

Think, Lantham. If you were wanting to pull this off, how

would you do it? A hologram? Too complicated. Expensive, not that that would worry anyone on the list of suspects except maybe Cynthia. Holograms need a medium—smoke or something   similar.   And   darkness— anything over a night light and they wash out to nothing. No, this was something else again.

What about basic theater tricks? A focused light and a gobo to create the shadow? A bright enough flash bulb, with a tight enough focus, could project a shadow that was just visible on an overcast winter day. And that would insure that everyone saw the same thing: a shadow that appeared, for a split second, to stand next to the car.

Question was, where?

Off to the left was a stand of trees, blocking the view of the main road, but that wouldn't do any good. When the car slid it was almost front-facing to the trees, the timing on the flash would have been impossible, and the foreshortening too wild. Besides, I remembered a flash that seemed to light up the whole car and a lot of the snow on the yard besides.

I closed my eyes and tried to play it back. From what angle did the flash hit the people on the lawn? I hadn't been looking at them, dammit. There went at least three thousand processor cycles wasted, and twenty seconds of cold too.

For the illusion to work from any angle—and it had to work from *any* angle; there was no way for the murderer to control for where everyone was standing—it would have to blast the car at nearly a right angle. I turned back to the skids, and looked dead at the twelve o'clock. Almost, but not quite, straight up the driveway to the garage.

Not that figuring out the illusion got me any closer to how the murder was actually done. A hell of a thing, pulling off a sideways slide in a sports car on a clean, dry driveway, and at just the right time that it would look like the ghost did it. And at just the right spot where it would land on the kids playset, guaranteeing death rather than just serious injury.

I swept the Mag-Lite once more across the lawn, to see if I missed anything. Survey says: nope.

One step onto the flagstone.

Crunch.

Not the crunch of a crumple zone like the one that started my weekend, but the crunch of gravel underfoot.

Gravel?

I shined the light down. A few stray white pebbles, right where the car slid. In a yard that didn't use pebbles or white river rocks for landscaping. Odd.

I picked one up and eyed it in the Mag-Lite. Rock salt.

"Oh, that's clever. Very clever." I swept the light over the ground, but only found a couple handfuls worth strewn on the pavement. That would be the work of the ghost, then—Sarah hadn't been seeing things, and that put a few more points on the graph.

A quick trip up to the garage, and with any luck I could wrap this up before breakfast without having to slog through all those documents.

To be safe, I kept the flashlight pointed at the ground in front of my feet. Flagstone, not concrete. Light slate greens and grays set out in an almost-regular pattern. Unnaturally clean, as if somebody polished it every day.

With the occasional darkish dot.

One or two at first, but more frequent the closer I got to the house. I scuffed at one of the dots.

It streaked. I bent over and picked some up on my fingers. Oily, but not engine oil—the consistency wasn't right. Neither was the color. This stuff was lightweight, the color of cheap olive oil—pale yellowy green.

Brake fluid. Our killer was a belt-and-suspenders kind of

schemer. That amount of dripping, the line would have a good healthy hole in it.

Up near the garage, where the car hadn't hit speed yet, it looked like a fairly steady trickle. If the hole had been in the brake line rather than a cylinder—brake lines are easier to get to—it was recent: the line hadn't bled out. Maybe poked the night before in the right spot.

I reached the garage. No way in from outside without the remote, I'd have to go round the inside if I wanted to check out any more of the fluid mess.

So, what was I looking for? Couldn't have been a video projector. Even a good one doesn't throw enough light to be useful at that distance in broad daylight—or, in this case, given the dimness of the overcast, narrow daylight.

No, we were looking for an ultra high-voltage camera strobe with a snoot. And maybe something to trigger it.

A look back at the crash site. Unless this was an elaborate suicide—a possibility I had to at least consider, though I hated giving Sam that much credit—the killer couldn't have known when Sam would go for a drive, or exactly how fast he'd be moving. There would be no dependable way to be in position to trigger the flash, and the timing would have to be perfect, maybe too perfect for a human to reliably eyeball it. I made his speed at the turn at maybe forty miles-an-hour—a little less than sixty feet per second, that made it precision work. Better to have a mechanical trigger.

A wire was out. So was a pressure plate. To much risk that someone would find those. But an IR trip could work. When the car broke the beam, it would trigger the flash. That would need a reflector.

For safety, I swept the front and side of the house, looking for the set-up. If this had been a suicide, Sam wouldn't have been around to strike the equipment.

No dice—though he could have set it up inside. There were two windows right at the corner, best place to set up. If the snoot were pressed right against the glass...

Yeah, that just might work.

I flashed the crash site again, sweeping for a reflector. Nothing. But if it had been concealed in the hedge...

A quick jog down. Root through the smashed hedges, broken twigs. Anything that looked like...

Yes. Smart. A pale bicycle reflector. In a house with kids, any cops coming across it wouldn't think anything of it.

Now, which window had the flash?

Starting at the front door, I counted off the paces to the door at the house's southwest corner. Twenty yards, only a few seconds at a dash.

The room looked like an old-style smoking lounge. Deep stiff-pile carpet, several French modern chaise lounges and a leather easy chair arrayed around a conversation pit. Cabinet humidor on one side. Soft lighting from lamps on tables arrayed between the seats. A room for entertaining, not the kind of room you use very often. Clean though. You could eat French fries, or French silk pie, or French maid off the floor if one were handy.

I walked around the outside of the room, along the least direct route to the windows I could find, to be sure I didn't disturb anything in case I found what I was looking for.

The room had two windows. The one nearest the edge of the house had three tell-tale imprints in it, from a tripod. Good deep marks—a heavy one, or mounting something heavy. Like a Xenon flash rig with a portable heavy-duty capacitor. About thirty pounds with good equipment.

Mounted right, an adult could move it as one piece, which at least pushed the kids of the list of suspects. Would've been some comfort if they'd actually been on it in the first place.

I had my method—one that removed the need for opportunity. It also scratched at least one of the adult suspects off the list. Sam didn't off himself—he wasn't around to play roadie afterward. Now, I just had to figure out which motive stood up.

BACK AT THE PORTABLE PRISON that people benignly call "computer," and my eyes were starting to go. Four in the morning. Another four hours until I had to meet my taxi for the trip to court. Most of what I'd spent the wee hours poring over was way beyond me—I knew enough about bookkeeping and how the investment banking game worked to spot some of the monkey business that Tom had mentioned. Lots of deals leveraged out to many ten thousands of percentage points. One bad deal and he could take the whole company down with him—try as I might, I couldn't find a bad deal in his books, but that didn't mean he didn't have them hidden somewhere else.

A whole bunch of stuff from upper management—V.P. Level and above. Naughty boy, my brother. Snooping on his bosses. And a half-finished letter to the SEC, looked like it never got sent. Not exactly slick.

He'd at least tried to covered his ass on insider trading. Judging by the rest of the security measures on his system (the passwords for the databases were made up completely of his kid's birthdays), he'd probably done it by just deleting his emails, so the DOJ could probably still get to them. Hell, I could get to them if I had a couple days alone with the system and the right toolkit.

An amateur-playing-professional white-collar criminal. If he hadn't died yesterday, he'd have been hanging from someone's gibbet by this time next year.

But that wasn't the most interesting part. Not by a long

way. Not by a bucketful of chocolate penises at the Folsom Street Fair.

No, indeed. The most interesting part was the log sheet he kept:

Sept 5. I'm keeping this log on the advice of my attorney. For some time now S's book club events have stretched to several hours. Suspect an affair. Tonight, she spent 6hrs out when meeting was sched 1hr. When she returned, informed me that she will not attend marriage counseling.

Sept 15. Caught Jimmy beating up on Sarah. Had to physically remove him. Would not listen. Said S. told him I was not his father and couldn't tell him what to do.

Sept 17. Argument with S. She has moved to her own room. Continues to undermine me in front of children.

Oct 1. Think S. is on the verge of a nervous breakdown. Not eating well, very moody. Screaming profanity when in empty rooms. Will not speak to me.

Oct 14. Several calls from household staff to office. S. has spent day drinking, refuses to speak to anyone. Children beside themselves. Have offered Cynthia extra money to assume au pair role for time being.

It went on like that for a long time. One, two entries a week. With all this going on, why hadn't he tried to divorce her?

Well, this was Sam. He'd have died to save his street cred as a good family man.

Maybe he did.

But that all changed in early December:

Dec 1. S called at work. Insists the house is haunted. Living room possessed. Informed me she is going to the diocese to ask for an exorcist.

Dec. 2. Exorcist visited house today. Found no cause for alarm. S. is apoplectic. Have instructed Cynthia to buffer her from the children.

Very Dickensian. Most appropriate for a Christmas story.

I couldn't help hoping that family friends would remember me and my sisters as proper Lanthams, and discount Sam and his house of idiocy as a one-off.

When I sifted through his web history, that hope turned to determination.

My darling brother, champion of the family name, received a shipment from Radio Shack on the eighth of November. The email receipt listed two long-throw ten inch subwoofers.

Wrench, meet monkey. Monkey, thy name is Lantham.

Sam faked the haunting?

I skimmed down the concordance until I found the words "haunting" and "infrasound." Yup. He'd read the papers. Downloaded them to his hard drive. All in late September.

So if Sam faked the haunting...who the hell had killed him? If he faked it so he had grounds to grab custody on the grounds that Samantha was mentally unfit, he wouldn't have killed himself.

Clarke Lantham, meet square one.

Brain, meet fatigue wall.

I set the alarm on my cell phone and laid down. Maybe a power nap would help me untie the knots.

6:00 AM, TUESDAY

THE TIME IS SIX AM. This is the time when naughty Lanthams drag their carcasses off the living room couch, upstairs for a shower, and then break out the best of what they have in their garment bag to go off to court.

Best to bring the phone and laptop too, with all the photos of the accident damage, including the position of the car, and the clandestine recording of the encounter with the cop, just in case. Not admissible as evidence, but at a pre-trial hearing, it might be useful to convince the prosecutor to lay off.

That, and a couple other entries in my bag of tricks, saw me safe to the taxi. I had it pick me up outside the main gate, so I could double-check that nobody had cleared away the rock salt, or the reflector, or the brake fluid drippings on the driveway.

Good so far.

I snapped a couple more photos on the way down—for safety, I kept my phone concealed from the house, and didn't stop walking. The overcast had broken enough that the shots came out intelligible, without appreciable motion blur.

NEWS TO ME, BUT SeaTac is actually a proper city with its

own courthouse. I'd always thought it was just the name of the airport, now I knew better—a fact which I filed away in the cabinet marked "information I hope I never need again."

Nice architecture for the period, but nothing special in the annals of public buildings. I spent an hour waiting in the hall 'til they opened the courthouse—course, if I'd shown up even five minutes late, I'd have found that they'd opened early and I'd have already drawn a contempt charge, but that was all down to Murphy, patron saint of the Lantham family.

Yeah, it was that kind of morning.

I killed some time on the net, digging up what I could on Sam's house. Built in the twenties by a former governor, sold to another, sold on to a third. Guess who never owned it? *Gangsters? Boy oh boy, Sam, I gotta hand it to you, you did a good job with your last con.*

'Twas the day after Christmas, and all through the courthouse, not a schedule was keeping, except for the louse. For what to my wondering eyes should appear, but Officer Bellman, the jerk of Ranier. He plopped down beside me and said something which I had to translate from belch to English.

"Still here, Cali boy?"

So he hadn't been having a bad day on Friday, he was a full-time poseur. Figured.

"How could I resist more time in your fair city?"

"Oh, you'll get plenty more time, my friend." He pulled a copy of a catalog posing as a news magazine out of his back pocket and started flipping through it. "This thing won't go to trial for at least a month."

Nice windup. I knew a shakedown when I heard one—or he was just hurting for ego points because he drank too much and couldn't get it up after Christmas dinner? He had that kind of gut that only chronic alcoholics get. "Nice Christmas?"

He chuckled. "It will be after I get your fruity ass back in jail where it belongs." This guy must've been molested by the Golden Gate Bridge as a child. And enjoyed it less than the rest of us did.

"What would you say if I told you I could get you promoted to detective?"

He chuckled again and read the magazine at me.

"Big splash." I almost dangled the possibility of his name in the papers, but Seattle hadn't actually had a paper newspaper in years. "Probably get you a feature story on MSNBC."

"You couldn't talk yourself out of a paper bag with a box of matches."

"Maybe. Or maybe I've just solved a murder up on snob hill and need a cop to take down the bad guy."

"Ha. You're a lying sack of..."

"Hand to God. Nothing says it can't be you that brings in a murderer today. Nothing says it can't be you that gets the credit for solving the case."

Yup, bucking for ego points. He took a bit of convincing, but one thing about big fish in small ponds: They're always willing to trade up for bigger bait.

The DA was willing to play ball too. I wound up in court all morning, but not at the hearing I came in for. I submitted my evidence, showed my retirement shield and my license—for credibility only. It wasn't valid outside California, but since I wasn't on a hire job (I conveniently didn't mention my niece's twenty-five cent retainer) the notion that I might offend a legislator didn't upset me—and told them what to look for on their warrant. The only other thing they needed was a suspect, and that's where I fell down a bit.

Still, a short list is better than no list at all. The DA's office promised to get in touch with homicide and send someone up in an hour or so. The chief consented to let Officer Bellman drive me back to the land of Lanthams-minus-one.

I don't care what you read about in Agatha Christie novels, no homicide department in the world lets private detectives carry out elaborate, group interrogations in order to finger the culprit. For one thing, it's not usually a good idea to let the suspect know *all* the evidence stacked against him before you charge him—there's always the possibility that you missed something, or he'll have time to enlist last-minute help to cover his ass. Worse, you could have the wrong guy, giving the real killer time to shore up his alibi.

For another thing, staged theatrics don't go over well in court, and it's very uncommon that you can extort a confession simply by cornering someone in front of their nearest-and-dearest. All in all, that kind of thing is a spectacular waste of time.

Of course, Officer Bellman didn't know this. He was a traffic cop who, until today, had only ever dreamed of wearing detective's duds. And I didn't suspect any of my putative relatives knew this either—so long as I'd known them, their lives had been so sheltered that the closest they came to violent crime was watching Brainy Smurf get kicked out of the village.

However, I hadn't gotten a Christmas present—I didn't count Sam's death. Disgust me though he did, dislike me though he had, I didn't actually hate him. I didn't count Cynthia's hospitality either, nice though it was.

Like I said, no Christmas present, and a whole lot of crap besides. This was payback. If I was going to get nothing else out of this weekend, I'd walk away knowing that I'd wrapped all the loose ends up nice and tight so that nobody—not Samantha, not Cynthia, not Tom and Edith, and definitely not the cops—would knock on my door once I got back home, except maybe to take the stand at the trial. Besides, it wouldn't *really* hurt anyone, leastways not the prosecution's case.

And since none of them knew any better, they all gathered in the living room, just like I—and the boar of a street cop standing behind me with the firearm—told them to. I set my phone on the table, with the audio recorder on.

"Sarah?" I knelt down in front of my niece, seated on her mother's lap at the end of the couch nearest the door. "Do you remember what you told me about the ghost?"

"Yeah."

"Tell me again what you saw on Christmas Eve?"

She looked at her knees. If she'd been standing, I'm sure she would have kicked at the ground.

"It's okay, sweetheart, just tell us what happened."

"I heard them."

"Them?"

"Voices shouting. Daddy yelling at someone. I got up and saw the ghost outside."

"How?"

Cynthia stepped in. "Her bed faces out the window."

"Ah, I see. So, what did you see, Sarah?"

"I…"

"It's okay. It's safe. The ghost can't hurt you."

"It killed Daddy." Oh, great. Well poisoning, anyone?

"Who told you that?"

"Grammie."

"Grammie is mistaken. Tell me what you saw."

Tom rolled his eyes. "Honestly, man, can you get to the point?"

"Officer Bellman, would you take Tom outside for a private chat?"

"My pleasure."

"No need, no need." Tom harrumphed, but didn't interfere further.

"Come on, sweetheart. What did you see?" I didn't actually

know what she was going to say, but I figured it might tell me something that could narrow the suspect list more.

"I saw the ghost, out by where Daddy crashed."

"Did you see what it was doing?"

She nodded.

"What was the ghost doing?"

"He...it...had a hose. It was watering the driveway."

Bingo. "Thank you, sweetheart, you can go play now."

Sarah slid off her mother's lap and trotted out of the room, stopping every couple steps to check with her mom and make sure it was okay to go. Once she was out, I turned to the boys. I picked Albert first—last thing I wanted to do at this stage was disrespect the pecking order.

"Albert, do you usually take the bus to church on Christmas morning?"

He shook his head.

"Why did you take the bus this time?"

"Uh...Mom wanted to."

"Oh?"

"Um..." he quick-checked Samantha, but didn't seem to get any help. "Yeah."

"Do you know why?"

"No, I..."

"Liar," Jimmy sneered, "We both saw him drinking in the study after breakfast. We took the bus so he wouldn't get us kil...um..."

I made a show of taking in the information. "Does he usually drink that much?"

"Not unless Mom and Dad are figh...ow!" Jimmy suffered an elbow to the ribs from his twenty-minutes-older brother. I reached in and hauled Albert off the couch before the scuffle could escalate.

"Albert, do you know what they were fighting about?"

He set his jaw, crossed his arms, and glared at me. "They weren't fighting."

"They were so. Fighting about us. Mom said she was gonna leave him and he was too much of a pussy..."

"Jimmy!" Samantha's ovaries decided to show up. Something vaguely comforting in that. It didn't slow him down though.

"...to keep her."

"He was not a pussy!" Albert ticked over into rage. I had to hold him back from jumping across the coffee table at his brother. "You take that back!"

"Shut up, dick face, he was so. A whiny drunk piece of crap pussy that hated us! He wasn't even our father, just pretended to be so he could order us aro..."

"Take that back, you jerk, or I'll pound you..."

"Boys!" Samantha stood up. "Stop it this instant." She was a mother, after all. She hit precisely that tenor of Mom-voice that even had me ready to snap to, at least for a split second. "Clarke, is this necessary?"

"Yes." I looked back at Albert. "Did you ever see the ghost?"

"No. But Mom did."

Samantha groaned.

"I know. Jimmy, did you?"

"No. But it's here."

"How do you know?"

"The hairs on my neck." He shuddered.

"Okay. You guys can go. If we need you again, I'll call. Stay in the house."

Without so much as an "okay," they both skulked as far as the doorway where Jimmy stopped.

"Sorry I called you a dick face."

Albert patted him on the back. "Sorry I hit you."

Jimmy returned the pat, then reached down and yanked Albert's underwear up so high that the poor kid's balls would probably decide not to drop for another year or two. "You're it, wedgie boy!" Jimmy dashed around the corner. Albert followed him, attempting to rearrange his underwear as he went.

"No running in the...house." Samantha gave up the shout halfway through.

I took a seat in one of the standalone chairs, leaned my elbows on the armrests, and tented my fingers. I dragged my gaze across each face. Samantha, overwrought—whether because she was rattled from her boys fighting, or because of last night, or yesterday, or because she was afraid of getting caught, I couldn't tell.

Edith, looking at the coffee table as if she could make the unpleasantness go away just by ignoring it.

Tom, arms crossed, left leg folded over his right, doing his best to look unamused. Confident. Determined. Combat pose.

And Cynthia, set apart from the family in the other chair. Suspense? Maybe expectant. Waiting to find out which shoe I was about to drop.

"Let me tell you what I know." I chose my words very deliberately, letting the space hang between them. "There is no ghost. And you," I nodded to Samantha, "Are not crazy."

"I saw it." Anger building under there.

"Yes, you did. You're not faking it, you're not crazy, and there is *no* ghost."

"But Sarah..."

"Sarah didn't see a ghost. She saw one of you." Blank faces all around. I brought my head up to rest on my fingertips. Time to up the ante. "So," I said, giving in to my most childish Poirot-fueled fantasy. "As you all know by now, there has been a murder. And one of you is a murderer."

"Preposterous." Tom fluffed himself up like an offended pigeon. Edith shifted her weight in a way that didn't reveal anything useful. Samantha fought back tears.

"Is it? What did we all see out there?" Test one.

Cynthia sat up a little straighter. "Sam drove over the cliff."

"No, not what happened, what did we *see?*"

"He came out of the garage," Samantha, talking like the words were only borrowing her voice box. "So fast. So loud. He got to the corner...turned onto the driveway...and the ghost...I swear, the ghost pushed the car sideways."

"Describe the ghost?"

"A...a shadow. Just a shadow. Oh, God..."

"You're not crazy. I saw it too."

"Me too." Cynthia said.

"Edith?"

She nodded.

"Tom?"

He shook his head. "I didn't see it. You sent me inside to make sure Sam didn't hurt the kids."

"No, I sent you inside to make sure he didn't do anything stupid. What did you see when you got inside?"

"I told you, he was already gone. I didn't see him, I didn't hear him yelling, so I went to find the kids."

"Samantha, what else do you remember?"

"I don't know...nothing. It's all a blur. It's like a slow motion movie."

"Wait. Wait, I remember." Cynthia pointed at Edith. "You ran out of the house yelling something. You ran out *before* Mister Lantham's car came out of the driveway. What were you..."

"You said 'Somebody stop him.'" Samantha shook her head slowly at her mother. "No, mama, no, you didn't...how did you know?"

"Know? I didn't know! He was drunk, he'd been drinking all morning. He stomped out of his office, tramped down to the garage. I tried to stop him but he pushed me out of the way." She looked at me, "This is your fault. He wouldn't have been in that car drunk if it wasn't for you. You were no good when you dated Samantha, and you're no good now."

"Edith, you're a perfect rose, thorns and all." I leaned back in the chair, "But this isn't my fault. No."

Her eyes were thin slits. Mama had teeth.

"Let's look at the facts. An Aston Martin DB9, one of the world's primo performance cars, rounds a corner that on any mountain road would be posted as safe for twenty or twenty-five miles per hour. It loses traction on the road and slides over a cliff? Not possible. The only way that car would go over a cliff is head-first. That wasn't a driving mistake. Not even my poodle could do that by accident." The fact that I'd never owned a poodle wasn't relevant, and they'd never find out anyway. "But that's okay, we all bought it, at least in the moment, because we saw the ghost push it off the road. A ghost with an overcoat and a hat like an old gangster. A lot of gangsters got killed here, right in this room, makes sense one of them would come back to haunt at some point, right?"

Samantha shivered.

"You thought so. You bought the whole story when you," I looked to Cynthia, "told her, after telling the kids gave them nightmares. It was a great story—perfect ghost story, except it wasn't true."

"What?" Cynthia's head snapped up.

"This house was never owned by a gangster. It was owned by a governor. No one ever reported a murder here—well, until now. Sam made that story up. He told me—he didn't know he was telling me at the time, just making small talk. Boasting about the historic landmark he lived in. He invented that story because he knew it would get around to Samantha.

"Sam wasn't a happy guy. He was miserable as a husband, even the kids knew it. He kept hitting on the hired help, even though you," I nodded at Cynthia, "would have clawed his eyes out. The DOJ was on his ass because of insider trading. You," I nodded at Tom "were after him for misusing company funds. You," I nodded at Samantha, "were determined to leave him and take the kids. But there's something about Sam none of you counted on, something he hid from you all the years he's been around."

"Oh, really, Mr. Lantham?" Tom was resorting to formality—something about this was getting to him. "What was this grand secret my son-in-law possessed?"

"Sam had a vindictive streak. He couldn't stand humiliation. If it came to it, he'd probably have tried to kill you, or you," I nodded at Samantha again, "rather than risk disgrace. But he didn't have to. He had a better plan. One that would let him walk away with all the cards, and keep the money.

"First, he'd turn state's evidence. His hard drive is filled to bursting with insider documents, stuff on upper management an investment manager shouldn't have. I'm no Arthur Anderson, but I'll bet you ten to one he had some dirt on you, Tom, and he was using it to cut a deal. Get you sent to jail as revenge for not promoting him fast enough, for hanging him out to dry, for making him get his own lawyer. But even better than that," I turned to Edith, "he'd take your grandkids away from you, and he'd do it by making sure you," I turned once again to Samantha, "would be declared an unfit mother."

They moped. Cynthia didn't. She was hooked. "How?"

"Last night I found a CD with an hour of infrasound on it. It's a trick sound engineers use in horror movies to make the hairs stand up on the back of your neck. Sam wired this place down by the heating ducts. Subwoofers. Then he set the CD to repeat, over and over. Any time someone took it out, he'd put it right back in. Maybe you saw it—a gold CD-R, no label? If you played it, all you got was silence?

"Except it wasn't silence, it just played sounds at frequencies too low for the human ear to hear. Long enough being droned with that, having it beat against your head day and night, and you'll start to swear something's in the shadows. Stand in a room where it's loud enough, and you'll see a gray shape in the corner of your eye, just from the vibrations you can't hear.

"He kept it up, making sure that Samantha got the lion's dose, so that when *he* filed for divorce, she'd look psychotic. He takes full custody. And keeps it. Game, set, match.

"Except that one of you liked the ghost story. Decided to use the haunting he engineered to cover up his murder. You knew he'd go out driving on Christmas to get away from the kids—that's the kind of asshole thing Sam would pull. He did it Saturday night too, after I got here—driving to work out his anger.

"So on Saturday night, long after he got back, you snuck out to prep the scene. About one o'clock. It took a while—at least until four. But it would, you had a lot to do.

"First, there was the black ice. Tricky thing, making sure it goes on in a clean sheet. You have to run the water really slow so you only cover the critical patch in the corner. One piece at a time, with no bubbles, until it was nice and thick. It was in the mid twenties, so it takes the water a while to freeze.

"Of course, that wasn't enough. There was always the possibility that the sun could come out and reflect so Tom would see it, so you needed a backup. You needed to be sure he couldn't stop short and ruin the whole thing, so you put a hole in the brake line. Tricky thing to do on a top-end car with only five inches ground clearance, but it worked. He left a brake fluid trail all down the driveway. Then you needed to take care of the ghost—a laser-trigger flash rig to cast a shadow at that range in broad daylight, not something that's easy to hide. I imagine it's still somewhere in the house. And you'd have to rig a reflector, so that when the car broke the beam the ghost would appear at precisely the right moment to push the car off the cliff, and right down on to the kid's playset. At that point, in a convertible, whether it landed on its side or rolled completely, nobody sitting under that rag top stood a chance.

"But once the deed was done, the nightmare wasn't over. You still had to clean up. Stow the flash rig until you could get it off the property. Dump rock salt in the driveway last night after dark, when no one would see you. Probably mop up the garage so the brake fluid would just look like old oil stains. But some of the rock salt didn't hit ice or snow, it's still out there. And you couldn't retrieve the beam reflector in all the confusion, or didn't think anyone would notice it buried in the crushed hedges. And you didn't think about the footprints the tripod would leave in the smoking lounge carpet."

Still not a reaction from any of them but Cynthia, who was absolutely riveted. All three of them must have had antifreeze for blood.

"That's a lot of work to be doing at night, two nights in a row. It would take a sociopath to do that and not be completely ragged during the day. But you had help, with some of it anyway. Jimmy had oil on his hands when we played laser tag. You got him to cut the brake line." Samantha gasped. Genuine horror, or I'm an idiot. Not that the two are mutually exclusive. "Makes sense—he didn't want to be taken away from his mother, and you probably told him it was just to scare his dad so he'd listen to reason."

I let it hang there. Nobody said anything for two minutes. I took a breath to start my windup, when a doorbell rang. "Officer Bellman, can you get that?"

"Hmph." He strode out, and returned in a moment with a pair of detectives and a forensics boy.

"Gentlemen, welcome. We were just getting to the juicy bit. If you can wait a minute."

"We want to ask..." The lead detective didn't get the sentence out of his mouth.

"Detective," said Bellman, "Give him a minute. Trust me."

"Very well."

"So, which one of us did it?" Cynthia didn't seem the slightest bit worried.

"I don't know. Oh, I have a theory, but I can't prove it. I don't have to prove it. All four of you already know who did it."

Four perplexed faces. "The person who did it wouldn't want anyone to know about the ice. So I'm guessing whoever first suggested taking the bus to church is the one who..." Three heads turned at once, in synchronized slow motion. All three sets of eyes focused right on Edith.

"No. No, I didn't." She didn't cower or shout, she didn't even stutter. She just looked around and defied everyone to come out and accuse her. I gave her what she wanted.

"It makes sense. You didn't want to see your grandchildren stolen. You've been around long enough, I'm sure you've seen some ugly divorces. You'd have the photo equipment for your roses."

"No."

"But you lost your nerve at the last minute. You tried to get us to stop him. I guess there's something in that, maybe."

"You cold-hearted bitch." Samantha whispered, like even saying the words was blasphemy.

"He'd been drinking that morning. Mimosas for breakfast and then in the study with..." she turned to Tom, "With you. You said neither of you were safe to drive. You made sure." Edith faced her husband, the disappointment on her face as profound as if she'd caught him in bed with a hooker. "No, Tom, please. Tell me you didn't do this."

Tom leaned forward on his elbows, dangled his hands below his knees, and drummed them together. "This is all circumstantial, Clarke. It'll never hold up in court."

"It will if Jimmy tells me who asked him to help play a prank on Sam."

Tom closed his eyes.

I pushed for my home run. "When you came into the house, you told him to take a drive and cool off, didn't you?"

"If you'll excuse me," he stood up, "I think it's time I called my lawyer."

I looked back at the detectives. "He's all yours, gentlemen. Please be sure Officer Bellman gets credit for the collar—without his help, I wouldn't have gotten to the bottom of it."

I collected my phone from the table, and, without turning off the recorder, I took it to the forensics officer. "Officer..."

"Macintosh."

"Officer Macintosh. This phone is recording this conversation. It's recorded everything that's been said in this room for the last half hour. Everyone saw me start it, they'll all testify to that in court. Can you verify that I handed this to you without shutting off the recording, and that you will now download the file directly so that I've had no chance to make any alterations?"

"Yes, certainly. This is Forensic Specialist Daryl Macintosh, and I have just been handed the phone exactly as described. To the best of my knowledge, contingent on witness testimony, the recording is genuine, made on the twenty-sixth of December at one-thirty P.M."

"Thank you. If you press the screen just there, you can terminate the recording."

Officer Bellman shoehorned his way in between the table and the sofa and took out his cuffs. "Thomas McIntyre, it is a distinct pleasure to place you under arrest for the murder of Samuel Lantham and for contributing to the delinquency of a minor in the commission of that crime. You have the right to remain silent..."

And so on.

1:45 PM, TUESDAY

I TOOK MACINTOSH THROUGH THE WHOLE CASE, made sure he had all the files and my contact info. I gave him the CD out of my laptop and, after checking the warrant, a dump of the USB stick with all the indexing I'd done. They'd have to do it again from Tom's computer to make it official, but nothing wrong with making their job a little easier. When a man kills your brother, it's what you gotta do, right?

It's what I kept telling myself, anyway.

Bellman gave me a lift to the airport on his way in to put Tom in lockup. The old man didn't say so much as two words the whole way, and I made sure to keep the conversation to things that he couldn't use to cloud the issue in court. No talk of the sweetheart deal that got me out of this mess in time to catch my flight.

I caught BART at the other end. Because I got bumped, they put me through SFO instead of Oakland. Still, on the way out I managed to charm my way through security so I didn't have TSA flunkies groping me. Just as well—I didn't want my last memory of the trip to be of some goose-stepping minimum wage moron with bureaucratically-inspired delusions of grandeur copping a feel. My penis deserved better treatment than that—it was my New Year's resolution.

Oakland in the winter has hills greener than the best eyes I've ever looked into. After a week and a half of colorless drab, it just about got me misty watching them through the train window.

Rather than have Rachael pick me up, or waste more money on a cab, I got off at Broadway and hoofed it the ten blocks through the drizzle. Worth it for the sheer novelty of having something fall out of the sky that wasn't fluffy and frozen.

With all the traffic and city smells and the odd bit of gang violence, it was good to be home.

The sun was setting bright red in the slit of sky between the cumulus clouds and peninsula mountains as I shouldered past a departing college kid and stepped through the front door. Angie—my downstairs neighbor—had already taken off for the day. I mounted the stairs one at a time, no rush, found the inauspicious door of Clarke Lantham Investigations right where I'd left it, still standing open.

Rachael was at her desk, pulling her hair out.

"I'm home."

"About damn time."

"Well there's a warm welcome. Shouldn't you be heading to your folks' for Christmas?"

"Couldn't leave the princess here alone."

"She can't be that bad."

"Really?" She raised an unamused eyebrow at me, then collected some papers and dropped them in a stack on the corner of the desk. "Merry Christmas. We've just been served. Seems like Dora Thales wants a piece of your hide. She's suing us for thirty million for malfeasance and wrongful death."

"Where's Nya?"

"Back in your office, watching a movie."

"Lovely."

On second thought, maybe Seattle wasn't so bad after all.

THE END
Clarke Lantham will return in
Smoke Rings

EXTRAS

ACKNOWLEDGMENTS

Several organizations and companies who make possible the world in which Lantham does his sleuthing bear mention, if for no other reason than they have trademarks on their names. In no particular order, they are:

Google, trademark owned by Google Inc.
Wikipedia, trademark owned by the Wikimedia Foundation
Brillo, trademark owned by Armala Brands
Star Trek, trademark owned by Paramount Pictures
Aston Martin, trademark owned by Aston Martin Motorcar Group
Bentley Motors, trademark owned by The Volkswagen Group
Ivory Soap, trademark owned by Proctor & Gamble Inc.

Thanks are due to many people who have, knowing and unknowing, been indispensable in helping create this little mystery. They are:

Kitty Nic'Iaian, who furnished invaluable editorial and graphic design assistance.

Beta readers Adam McCullough and Chris Lester, for catching continuity glitches.

Dean Wesley Smith and Kathryn Kristine Rusch, for a dare over dinner.

Huge thanks and gobs of appreciation to all the fans who've been pestering me to release this book since its first public reading earlier this year—I hope it lived up to expectations.

And finally, special thanks to Gail Carriger, for reasons best left a mystery in their own right.

Author's Note

Travel can broaden the mind. Depending on how much junk food you eat while on the road, it can widen the waistline. In my case, it also tends to thicken a book, or series of books.

I write on the road. At conventions you can often find me set up in the bar typing till my fingers fall off, or up late in the lobby after everyone's gone to sleep, happily rallying couches, chairs, coffee tables, and end tables under my banner. New faces, new places, and new adventures barge into my head and feed cheap pick-up lines to ideas I've been holding on to just in case they become useful, and those ideas, dirty sluts that they are, grab onto those new experiences and start fornicating furiously all over the room—hence the need for all the extra furniture in hotel lobbies.

The month after I released *And Then She Was Gone*, I took to the road with one of my best friends to conquer the great early-winter convention circuit in the Northwest. I was already starting to toy with starting the new Clarke Lantham adventure, which at that point was supposed to be *Silent Victor* (it's now book 4 in the series), when the road opened new possibilities.

As we crossed the border into Oregon I asked myself: "Self, what would happen to Lantham if he got caught in a mystery while out of state? He obviously couldn't act in a professional capacity—at least, not legally—so what would he do?" It wasn't a question I had a good answer to, but hey, it kept me awake for a half hour behind the wheel while my companion napped in the passenger seat.

Getting caught in the worst Seattle snowstorm in a decade, though, gave me what I really needed. So did the pickup truck that tried to drive over the little car we were in. Between ice, car crashes, sloped bridges, and all the misadventures they caused, it really was a trip to remember—and an exhausting day. By the end, when we reached our night's destination, I was ready to sleep—except I couldn't. As soon as I laid down I got visions of Lantham and car crashes in my head, so I pulled out my laptop and set it up on my bedside table and started thrashing at the keys.

Never underestimate the power of irritation to produce great mystery set-ups. Nor the power of misadventures to provide great laughs in the retelling.

The actual misadventures didn't make it into *A Ghostly Chrstmas Present*, but it's safe to say that the book never would have happened if it hadn't been for that lovely little encounter with a 4x4 on an icy road—or the day that followed, complete with its frustration, its problem-solving, and the ubiquitous laughter that comes from being stuck in hellish circumstances with the most excellent cohort anyone could ask for.

And for Lantham? He's got a lot more in store for him in the next few volumes. You won't want to miss it, because I swear you're not gonna believe the trouble he gets himself into just a couple days after getting back from his Seattle trip.

Till then...

–J. Daniel Sawyer
San Francisco, CA
April 2012

ABOUT THE AUTHOR

Even a respectable upbringing couldn't save J. Daniel Sawyer from a life of crime. As a high school hacker and serial trespasser, he often found himself the subject of unfriendly police attention. As a citizen unable to mind his own business, his frequent encounters with embezzlers, rapists, grifters, pornographers, corrupt public officials, murderers, and ice cream truck drivers around the San Francisco Bay provides him with endless source material and high doses of adrenaline.

After winding up on the wrong end of a gun once too often, he brought his sordid past as firearms instructor, security consultant, and INS detention contractor to bear on his hard-boiled *Clarke Lantham Mysteries*.

The author of thirteen books, including the award-nominated spy series *The Antithesis Progression* and the creepy comedy *Down From Ten*, he spends his down time searching the San Francisco back country for the ultimate driving road—and avoiding traffic cops.

For stories, contact info, podcasts, and more, visit his home page at
http://www.jdsawyer.net

If you enjoyed *A Ghostly Christmas Present*,
you might also enjoy the following sample of

Smoke Rings

Book Three of
J. Daniel Sawyer's
The Clarke Lantham Mysteries

8:00 PM, NEW YEAR'S EVE

I DIDN'T GO TO A NEW YEAR'S EVE party this year. Last year, I'd wound up at one where an impromptu murder spree broke out, and I'm not keen to repeat the experience. Aside from having to work on my day off—it takes the cops a while to get to a remote mountain cabin on New Year's eve, no matter how much the wildlife complains about the rude, lumbering bald monkeys cluttering up their 'hood—I also wound up losing a girlfriend I was getting pretty fond of: Kristine Warner, who I'd intended to propose to after the party died down. I would have, too, if those two bodies hadn't shown up.

Kris was the kind of woman who liked her lines clear, and liked to pay her debts. Saving her life from a knife-wielding maniac put her in a position she couldn't stand: she felt like she owed me. That was pretty much the last I saw of her.

Well, the last I saw of her in a social context, at any rate. I kept finding ways to bump into her on business grounds. She was happy to help out when I needed a doctor's input for a client—she liked paying her debts—but nothing else changed between us.

In the year since, I hadn't had time to make many dates. And I wasn't keen to head out on the town stag, or in the company of my assistant and my current penance project.

This New Year's Eve, I was determined to spend the time using my toes to polish the insides of my socks. It was the only time I'd have to myself in my office for the foreseeable future, and I knew it. My life had been wrecked a week back by dregs from an old case washing up on my doorstep in the form of the just-past-teenaged Nya Thales, a girl with more than a little bit going for her and a mother who has a psychotic interest in putting me in debt to the tune of seven figures because she doesn't like the way I shot her husband in order to save her daughter's life. The result of that particular family drama gives off a funk that's going to be hanging around for a long time yet.

At least I've got Rachael on the line now. At three-quarters-past twenty, she's taken to Nya like a recalcitrant older sister, if older sisters are allowed to kiss younger sisters like that when they're drunk. Not something they allowed in the town where I grew up. I've decided not to investigate too much in that direction. Besides, days off, right?

My plan for the day—or night—off: take the time to enjoy the fact that, for a few brief, fleeting moments, I wouldn't be dodging random gouts of post-teenage estrogen. Rachael had taken Nya out to some shindig in the city, and I didn't expect either of them would be stopping back here before the end of hangover hour tomorrow morning. I had a book to read that had nothing to do with law enforcement, a new bottle of scotch I planned on draining slowly over the next eight hours, and—an annual tradition—a bundle of Churchill-sized Excaliburs.

I don't normally smoke, but this one day a year, I take two in memory of the partner who taught me to blow smoke up the chief's ass and keep myself out of trouble. She was five-foot-two, fifty-eight years old, and talked like she'd just gotten out of the coyote's U-haul. She smoked like a chimney and blew rings that would hang in the air for three minutes if you didn't move, just spinning in the light.

Alexia Lopez. A hell of a brassy dame. She bought it when we were hunting the Broadway Slasher—took a corner too wide on Skyline when we were doing the take-down.

You can probably tell by now that I have a bit of a checkered relationship with the opposite sex. It's not of the "can't live with 'em, can't shoot 'em" variety. I'd happily shoot one that needed shooting, but I've been lucky enough that everyone I've had to plug so far has come equipped with the same plumbing I've got, so I don't get to add "post-feminist homicidal ex-cop anxiety" to my list of mental disorders. I think if I can nail that one and "hypochondriac male artist" to the scorecard, I can send off for a free set of luggage.

The rain outside my office window was coming down hard. Hard enough that the Oakland city lights shining through the normally wavy Victorian glass looked like sequins in skin-paint from an energetic burlesque routine. I poured myself the first glass of the night—for me, eight o'clock is the official start of drinking hour on New Year's Eve—and I raised it to the city beyond the window. "Here's to surviving one more trip around the sun. If one of us has to go, better you than me."

Don't get me wrong, I like living—or, as far as the city planning department knows, keeping an office—in Oakland, but it's a miserable town shot through with the kind of corruption you normally think they reserve for the movies. For the last five years I've been locked in a staring contest with it—one of these days, one of us will blink.

I sat there in the dark for a good piece, stocking feet on the window sill, lights out, back to the door. I'd left the light in the outer office on so I'd have a good view if anyone tried to bash the door down—I had a standing suspicion that one of these days another one of the characters from the Thales case was gonna bust through there with more lead pills than the RDA allows. If I was the kind of guy who actually slept at night, it might keep me up.

Wasn't going to happen tonight, I was pretty sure. Not in weather like this. I mean, would you want to be a hit man on New Year's Eve? And since I had a .45 and a .38 snub within arm's reach, I wasn't hurting for options.

Besides, it was my day off, and I had a bright year ahead of me. If you think it's a bit early to tell what kind of year I was going to have, you haven't been keeping up. I could spend the entire year investigating low-lifes trading kiddie porn like baseball cards and it wouldn't raise to half the level of weird, dark, and downright unpleasant I had to deal with last year. Actually, at this point, a handful of garden variety sickos would be a welcome relief.

Yeah. Good year. I could get used to this having-the-office-to-myself thing again. Even after a little less than a week, Nya was a sweet kid, but with a suffocating presence.

Speaking of suffocating...

I took one of the cigars and cut it, then warmed the end over half a match before sucking the fire from the other half into the business end. After the first few puffs, I got a good sized smoke ring to settle slow against the cold glass in the window frame and churn in place for about twenty seconds before the convection currents eroded it away into afterthoughts. Alexia would've been proud.

"Got another one?" A voice from behind me. One I hadn't heard in a while—one I'd only heard a few times since last New Year's Eve.

I didn't turn around, just looked into the window glass. Once I re-focused, I could see Kristine Warner standing in my front doorway.

"In the bag on the file cabinet." I didn't invite her to sit. The acknowledgment of her presence was enough.

She closed the front door behind her as silently as she'd

opened it, then soft-footed through my front office and into my inner sanctum, stopping at the file cabinet for the bag from the tobacco shop. A minute later, there were two fresh smoke rings dancing against the window-skin.

"Nice one. I didn't know you could do that."

"Same skillset," she said, "different tool," and she stuck the cigar into her mouth and sucked on it in a way that made me miss her all over again.

Nostalgia is a disease that hits widows, veterans, and old cops the way malaria hits naked sunbathers in the Congo. You'd think after what happened in Seattle last week I'd be pretty well vaccinated, but you'd be underestimating the size of my squishy underbelly. Good thing I didn't have to turn around to see the look on her face.

I took another drag—my third in as many minutes—and popped a series of small rings, like spitting wispy donuts that broke on the glass, scattering everything else away before clinging to the cold like fog.

"It's new year's eve," I said, "Shouldn't you be out at a party or anesthetizing someone or something?"

"Mmm. No point. I'm on call tonight." She had a job in the ICU at Children's Hospital. She preferred emergencies, worked like she was paying off karma—would've gotten in the way of our relationship when we were together, except that I work like I'm trying to keep from remembering something. We were a good match, once upon a time. "What are you drinking?"

"Macallan twelve." I reached down next to my chair, hooked the neck between my fingers, swung it around over my head to land it on the table behind me. "You remember where the glasses are. Don't turn the lights on."

She didn't reply, but I saw her reflection stand and make its way to the little kitchenette behind the chintzy Ikea rice paper screen at the north end of the office. There were some clinks while she tried to sort between coffee mugs and bar glass in the dark, then more footfalls across the brown-painted 1920s wood floor and up onto the throw rug. The scotch glugged in the glass. Usually one of my favorite sounds—right now it just sounded like someone stealing my solitude and handing me loneliness like they thought I didn't know the difference between the two.

I leaned forward to tap the first little bit of ash off the cigar. Excaliburs are finicky with their ash—prone to dropping it in big clumps without warning you. I once lost a perfectly serviceable tiger-print silk shirt that way.

"Pass that back here?"

I grumbled something about a perfectly serviceable trash can next to the desk, but I passed it back anyway. There was paper in the trash can, didn't really want to see the fire brigade tonight. I had all the fire I really wanted sitting on the end of six inches of thick-gauge portable coffee-and-vegetable tasting goodness.

Passing a full ash tray behind you when you're leaning back in an office chair with your socks on a window sill is a bit like trying to do the can-can in chain-mail, but I wasn't about to turn around and look at her. After a whole year, she could still make the fluid drain out of my throat and dance around in my stomach. To share a room with Kristine Warner is to live in that first weightless second at the top of a very high roller coaster for hours on end.

Time was, once, that I thought I'd eventually get to have a normal life. There'd be a girl—or, as I edged past thirty, a woman—who could deal with being married to a whack-job like me. There'd been a few along the way, but it wasn't until Kris that I really believed it wasn't a pipe dream. When she threw me over, she'd taken that last bit of hope I had that I'd get to have a normal life someday, put its teeth upon the curb, and stomped it until its skull cracked like an egg. Maybe she needed to find a way to forgive me for saving her life. I was never going to forgive her for breaking my heart.

You'd think that would stop me from wanting to turn around and tear her shirt off and start the new year with a bang, wouldn't you?

So would I, except I was in the room with her, living at the top of that roller coaster, and I could still remember the way her sweat cut through the smell of the cigar like perfume. In between drags I could taste her skin, the soft way her lips always seemed like they were made of of white chocolate, the way her nipples reminded me of raisins when they tightened from pink to dark brown, even now, a year after the last time I'd seen her in anything less decent that jeans and a sweatshirt. And I hated her for it.

Which is why I didn't turn around to look at her. I just talked to her reflection. "Drinking when you're on call?"

"Special occasion."

"Your malpractice insurance is gonna love that when you drop a kid on its head."

"Fuck you." She set the tumbler on the desk, picked her cigar up from the ash tray, and proceeded to poke me with visual reminders of why her diction was so precise.

I squinted at her reflection. Trouble was, she had the kind of poker face that kept me interested for the two years we were together—which gives her an unmatched Lantham record—and she'd only gotten better in the year since. Studying her wasn't doing me any good. Still, I wasn't eager to end the silence. The only thing worse than her face was her voice.

But the cigar was smoldering half-way down, and it's a two hour cigar. My hips were getting achy sticking in one position for too long—one of the side effects of aging that leads me to tell my sister's kid that he needs to find some really bitchin' way to die before he hits thirty—and if she didn't say something soon I was going to have to shoot her, just on principle. Or at least what passed for principles in my world.

The one thing I had on her, though, was patience. I do stakeouts for a living, she only has to wait for blood tests to come back. It's a close contest, but in waiting games, I always won. Drove her nuts.

I won this time, too.

"Good cigar." She blew another smoke ring.

"Yup."

"How've things been? You know, around here?" She waved an airy hand at my makeshift domicile. I was suddenly glad that Nya hadn't left her underwear to line dry over the radiator this evening.

"Things are fine. Business is good." The English language is vague, and "good" is a very fluid term. My lawyer's wallet was doing good extremely well, and I was doing good enough to keep it from starving, barely. None of my longstanding bill collector relationships had progressed to the "baseball bat" stage. Of course, I was now carrying one assistant and one stray, so what constituted a healthy income had taken a turn toward "ouch" territory. What are you fishing for, Kris? Let's get it out of the way so I can enjoy my depressingly celibate New Year's Eve.

"Got any plans for the evening?"

"None that you're not currently wrecking."

"What, you were going to sit here drinking and smoking till the sun came up?"

"I've got a chow mien and masturbation break scheduled for 3:30 AM, but other than that, yes. That was the general idea."

She set her cigar down like a woman with something on

her mind. "I've got a better idea."

"I was already circumcised against my will by one of your kind. Forgive me if I don't come over all gushy and trusting."

"Women?"

"Doctors."

"Ah."

Now, I'm the kind of guy who hears sentences like *Lantham, your check just bounced* pretty often. Sentences like *Lantham, the toilet's just backed up and overflowed the plumbing*, or *Lantham, why is there a dead hooker in your bedroom?* or *Hand over the pictures or the girl gets it* aren't unheard-of. So you'll understand what I mean when I say that I just about snarfed my scotch through my nose when she said what she said next:

"Actually, I came by to invite you to a New Year's Eve party."

"Right." *And I've got a bright green tattoo of George W. Bush snorting cocaine with the Pope on my chest.*

"I mean it."

"Mmm." I sucked on the cigar, took my time making a ring, letting the smoke cool down so it would hold together properly.

"And where, pray tell, is this mythical New Year's Eve party?"

"Santa Clara Convention Center."

"At this hour? On New Year's Eve?"

"Can you think of a better time for a New Year's Eve party?"

"How about when neither of us has been drinking." The convention center was at the Hyatt near the used-to-be-kinda-Great America amusement park—about forty miles south of my tragically over-occupied office. The CHP and the locals were all pretty humorless on nights like tonight.

She picked up the bottle and examined its level. "You've

only had one. You're fine."

"This is your considered medical opinion?" I put my tumbler aside—not quite finished yet—just in case I'd need to go driving.

"I don't have any other kinds."

"That's not how I remember it." I growled, and meant it. She was officially overstaying her welcome now. Ambivalence cocktails have a short shelf life before they turn completely sour, and the one she poured when she walked through the door was starting to smell like turpentine.

"Hey now..."

"Hey now yourself. What the hell are you really doing here?"

"Me?" It wasn't coy and innocent. More like she was collecting her thoughts and screwing up her courage. I added it to the list of things she'd screwed up. "I wanted to make up for last year."

"Trust me, Kris. *Nothing* could make up for the last year."

"Not the last year. Last year. One year ago tonight."

"You weren't the one killing party guests."

"Goddammit...just let it go, will you?"

"What, that you dumped me because I saved your life?"

"Fuck you."

"That would be an improvement."

"Look, I'm sorry..."

"You and the fucking Pope."

"Are we going to have this fight *again?*"

"No, not again. Still. This fight is all we've got." I was getting surly now. "You're the one who walked through that door and wrecked my evening. You can damn well walk back out again."

"Fine." She stood up and brushed her hair back like she was making sure she still had her dignity with her. "You just remember that you're the one who slammed the door on a fifty-thousand dollar payday."

"Say what?" Socks are fickle creatures with minds of their own. Mine chose that moment to give up their grip on the window sill. I scrambled to keep from dropping my cigar, barely managed to keep hot coals from falling onto my shirt. It emerged uninjured. My poker face, however, was mortally wounded and limped away to cough up blood in the corner. I spun in my chair and stared at her in open incredulity. "Fifty thousand? What the hell..."

She was already at the door to my inner sanctum, the light of the outer office wreathing her in a yellow halo. She half-turned back to me, and I thought I saw the side of her mouth twitch, like it wanted to smile.

"So you are interested."

"When you put that many zeros next to each other..."

"You say that now..."

"Cut it out. What are you talking about?"

She shrugged. "It was gonna be a surprise." She shook her head a little bit, like she was trying to decide whether to spoil it. Something else, hard to identify, fluttered across her face. Regret? Disappointment? Hard to be sure, but it wasn't good.

Lantham, you asshole, she wanted you to come because you wanted her, not because you wanted the money. The icy realization clutched my stomach. I'd just blown my chance to patch things up, the chance I'd wished for all year. Now it was all business. And when it was done, whatever it was, she'd consider her debt paid, and I wouldn't see any more of her.

I said earlier that I'm not the swiftest canary where women are concerned. In this case, I was playing for last place in a tortoise race—it wasn't until that moment that I realized that I still loved her.

You don't get very far in this business by "listening to your heart." You get ahead—and stay alive—listening to your interpersonal radar and your wallet, and then occasionally throwing a glance over at your conscience to make sure it's not throwing up all over your best suit. You listen to your heart, you're liable to drive your wallet, your conscience, and your business all out onto the street to pace back and forth with cardboard signs saying "Will work for anyone who's not a chump."

Fifty thousand. That's a five with four zeros after it. Not counting the Beatles, anything with four or more zeros is officially worth my time, even on vacation. Even on New Year's Eve.

"Oh, it's a surprise. Third one tonight. You remember how I love surprises." She'd once surprised me by yanking the string on a party popper behind my back when I didn't know she was there. I was having a bad day, had just got in from a shouting match with the local deputy, so my hackles were up. If I wasn't in the habit of carrying my weapon with the safety catch on, I'd probably have shot her.

She rolled her eyes and sighed. "Look, it's worth it, okay? Trust me. I'll tell you on the way."

"Assuming we're not going to a 'who looks the most like Sam Spade' contest to compete for the prize," I crossed my arms over my chest and stuck my legs, one at a time, up onto the corner of my desk, "I'm gonna need to know the score so I know what toys to bring."

That faint smile again. Maybe with some relief? Hard to tell. But she turned back to face me, walking forward into rippling rainlight. She took a seat, leaned forward so I could smell her again. I had to take a French lit class in college once—believe me, Proust had a gift for understatement. Seemed like every memory connected to Kristine came flooding back at once.

But I didn't blink. I just listened to my wallet.

She propped her elbows on the desk. "Have you heard of Giles Noyce?"

I shrugged and shook my head. "Vaguely rings a bell."

"One of the FBI's most wanted. A medical insurance guy. He was an accounts manager who ran a Ponzi scheme on some patients a few years ago, disappeared when he was indicted by a grand jury. Killed a teenager in a hit-and-run trying to get out of town."

"Cool." If you're from the Bay Area, this is one of those words that, depending on your inflection, can mean anything from "Oh my god that's the greatest thing ever" to "I can't believe you're wasting my time with this." My response fell somewhere on the unenthused end of the spectrum.

"There's a fifty thousand dollar price on his head."

"Standard FBI reward?"

"Yeah."

"So, what about him?"

"Well, I can't be sure, but I think he's back in town. He's been in and out of the hospital in the last couple weeks, and I recognized him from his post-office pictures. Him or someone who looks a lot like him."

"And he's going to be at this party?"

"The company he's working for is giving it. He invited a few of us—I think he was picking up on me." Could blame him for that, but I wasn't going to say it out loud. "So I thought that if you could ID him, you could get the reward."

Yup. She was after payback. Get me off her conscience.

Still, fifty K is nothing to sneeze at, and nabbing white collar criminals is a hobby I don't get to indulge near often enough.

"It's already after nine. New Year's Eve parties start to wind down around midnight..."

"Oh, don't worry about that. A couple of my girlfriends are already there, they say it's going to last till dawn."

A setup like that is hard to turn down. I took another hit on the cigar, made a show of chewing the proposition over while I made a mental list of the toy box I'd need to pack.

She watched me like she was trying to read my mind. I used to love it when she looked at me that way.

After a couple minutes, I stubbed out the cigar. "Give me five minutes to pack. Do you know if he's got a room there? No, forget it, you wouldn't. Let's bet he does. Let's see...stand up for a second, will you?"

She did. I studied her. Stood up and walked around, looking at her from all angles. "First thing, we're gonna need to get you out of those clothes."

Get the rest of
Smoke Rings
in paperback or ebook at *www.jdsawyer.net*
or wherever books are sold